RAKE MOST LIKELY TO SIN

Bronwyn Scott

Bronwyn Scott is a communications instructor at Pierce College in the United States, and is the proud mother of three wonderful children (one boy and two girls). When she's not teaching or writing she enjoys playing the piano, travelling—especially to Florence, Italy—and studying history and foreign languages. Readers can stay in touch on Bronwyn's website, bronwynnscott.com, or at her blog, bronwynswriting.blogspot.com. She loves to hear from readers.

Books by Bronwyn Scott

Mills & Boon Historical Romance
and Mills & Boon Historical *Undone!* eBooks

Rakes on Tour

Rake Most Likely to Rebel
Rake Most Likely to Thrill
Rake Most Likely to Seduce
Rake Most Likely to Sin

Rakes of the Caribbean

Playing the Rake's Game
Breaking the Rake's Rules
Craving the Rake's Touch (Undone!)

Rakes Who Make Husbands Jealous

Secrets of a Gentleman Escort
London's Most Wanted Rake
An Officer But No Gentleman (Undone!)
A Most Indecent Gentleman (Undone!)

Ladies of Impropriety

A Lady Risks All
A Lady Dares
A Lady Seduces (Undone!)

M&B *Castonbury Park* Regency mini-series

Unbefitting a Lady

Visit the Author Profile page
at millsandboon.co.uk for more titles.

For Pong and Louis, our fabulous servers on the Magic.
Thanks for making our voyage with you spectacular!
This was an unforgettable trip to unforgettable places.

Chapter One

Dover—March 1835

Lucifer's bloody balls! Was that the time? Brennan Carr reached one arm out of bed and snatched his watch up from the crude table to be sure. He angled the pocket watch to catch what little light was in the room and peered at the watch face. He groaned and fell back on his pillows. It bloody well was. His ship sailed in less than an hour and it wasn't even daylight yet. Brennan scrubbed a hand over his face. Where had the night gone?

Beside him, the luscious Sarah—no, that wasn't right, close, but not right—Sylvia? Serena? Cynthia! That was it. The luscious *Cynthia* stirred and raised herself up on one arm, her other hand exploring under the blankets until she found what she was looking for. She closed a firm, warm hand over his cock. 'Ah, lovey, like that, is it? You're ready for li'l ol' Cynthia again.' She smiled in the dark, her long blonde hair falling over one shoulder. She executed a smooth move that had her straddling him. 'Lucky for you, Cynthia is ready, too.' She giggled at referring to herself in the third person. She sat atop him, scooping her extraordinarily well-endowed breasts into her hands and rubbing them together. 'Cynthia's bubbies want you to suck them.'

Brennan blinked. That confirmed it. He must be brutally sober because he distinctly remembered the third-person bit being as funny as hell last night after copious quantities of ale in the taproom, but the hilarity had gone. He was going to be late and being late meant missing the boat. His body might still be enchanted with Cynthia's charms, but his mind was done with her. He had no desire this morning to prove true the old adage about time and tide waiting for no man.

His travelling companions would worry, especially Haviland. For the past twelve years of their friendship, it had been Haviland's job to worry about him, but he'd promised himself he'd do better on this trip, give Haviland less to worry about. He would prove he was an adult. So far, only three days out from London, he hadn't done a very good job.

Brennan politely dislodged Cynthia. 'I'm sorry, I have to leave.'

Cynthia grabbed his arm and rolled a leg on top of his. She pouted with full lips. 'Not yet, you can go one more time with Cynthia. No one has to be anywhere this time of day.'

'I do.' He tried to move away, but she held fast, resolutely ignoring the clues that he was finished. It wasn't that he couldn't overpower her but he didn't want to make a scene. He'd rather leave politely. Scenes tended to ruin the memories of pleasure that preceded them and Brennan loved pleasure above all else. But Cynthia was surprisingly strong and increasingly tenacious, or desperate.

'Really, you can't go yet.' She smiled brightly and reached for the tie holding back the bed curtains. 'We could try ropes. We haven't done that yet.' She yanked, the tie coming loose in her hands. 'I could get Mary from the room next door. She wanted a go with you, too. She could…'

Brennan didn't wait to hear what Mary could do. He leapt up from the bed, pushing Cynthia aside, no longer caring about her sensibilities. It was definitely past time to go. He was starting to divine there was more at play here than a pouting seamstress wanting one more tup before she returned to the shop. He reached for his clothes, shoving his legs through his trousers with haste.

Cynthia rose from the bed, gloriously nude—it was hard not to be distracted— and she might have been successful in keeping him if it hadn't been for that look in her eye—a hard, calculated look that said the time for games had gone. 'Surely you aren't going to leave without paying poor Cynthia. She gave you the whole night.'

Brennan's fingers stopped on his shirt buttons. Pay her? She was a whore? 'You said you were a seamstress, that all of you worked at the dress shop.' He remembered that very plainly.

The three girls had come into the dining room of the hotel, smiling and flirting with him and his friends. Nolan had humoured them before going off to play cards. Archer had followed Nolan as usual. The 'ladies' had left after that, trading the genteel dining room for the adjoining taproom. He'd run into them there. Idiot! That should have been his first clue; Women in the taproom. There was only one sort of woman who frequented taprooms.

'Seamstress by day.' Cynthia closed in on him, advancing. 'Cynthia has to support herself somehow. This room doesn't come cheap.'

They'd come here around midnight. She'd explained it was her quarters, just a few streets from the hotel. Brennan hopped into his boots, tugging them up. How was he to tell her he hadn't any money on him? Everything was packed safely away in his trunk on board ship. That brought on a whole new wave of panic. If he missed the boat, he'd be cut off from all of his support: clothes, money, everything. All he'd have would be quite literally the clothes on his back.

Brennan held his arms out wide in a gesture of contrition and tried a handsome smile. 'I misunderstood the nature of our association, Cynthia. I never took you for a lady of the evening.' He used the most delicate term he could think of for her occupation. Perhaps she would see the compliment he intended. 'We did have a nice time. I had some pleasure, you had some pleasure.' He knew that much was true. She'd liked him. No one was that good at faking it and he had what might be called an 'excellent track record' at supplying pleasurable experiences. He was sure last night had been no hardship for her. 'Why don't we call it square?' He edged towards the door, scooping up his pocketwatch from the table. Too late, he remembered his greatcoat laying over the chair across the room. He thought about crossing the chamber to get it. That was when she screamed.

And screamed.

And screamed some more. She was going to wake the entire building. Which of course was exactly what she intended. His greatcoat would have to be sacrificed.

Brennan threw open the door and shot a

look down the hall both directions. People were peering out of their rooms as he bolted towards the stairs. He could hear Cynthia behind him, screaming specific names now—names like Jake, which he thought might belong to some sort of protector. Halfway down the stairs, he heard boots behind him; two men in varying states of undress in pursuit.

Thankfully the wharf wasn't far. He hadn't the coin for a carriage even if there was one to be had. Brennan sprinted out into the morning, nearly colliding with a man delivering fruit to the hotel the next street over. 'Which way to the docks?' he gasped out.

He ran, following his nose down alleys and narrow streets, as long as they led towards water. The men behind him followed. *You'll make it, you'll make it...you always do.* The mantra coursed through his brain as his legs pumped. This wasn't the first time he'd been pursued by angry husbands, brothers or other upset male relatives.

He made the wharf and then realised he had no idea which ship was his. Haviland had made all the arrangements and, as usual, Brennan had not listened. Haviland took care of everything, all he had to do was show up. And he hadn't even quite managed to do that, yet.

It was harder to run on the docks. They were crowded with people and cargo waiting to be loaded. He dodged around crates and wagons. A few drivers called out curses as he spooked their horses with his sudden presence. He darted in and out of people carrying sacks of grain. Every so often, he glanced over his shoulder to see if he was still followed. He was horrified to note one of his pursuers had drawn a pistol, no doubt sensing the chase was ending. And it was. He would reach the end of the dock. If he didn't find the ship, he would be finished. There'd be nowhere else to run.

He heard shouts and looked out towards the far point of the dock. Three men stood at the rail of the ship just beginning to push off from the dock. One of them was waving madly, tall and commanding, his greatcoat flapping in the morning breeze. Haviland! Brennan would recognise that posture of control anywhere. Behind Haviland, Archer and Nolan raced the length of the rail, making wild gestures to something behind him. Archer was yelling full sentences worth of words, but Brennan could only make out one word, Archer's favourite word: horse. It didn't make sense. What would a free-running horse be doing here? On cue there was the pounding of hooves, the heavy thunderous breathing of a horse in full gallop and then the horse was beside him, matching his stride to Brennan's.

'Get on! Get on!' Archer cried, cupping his hands around his mouth. Brennan knew instantly what to do. He didn't stop to think, thinking had never done much for him and now was not the time to re-examine its usefulness.

He grabbed mane and swung up on the horse's bare back. There was twenty feet to the edge of the dock and then the leap. Brennan didn't think of the consequences if he missed, or the impossibility of making the jump. This was nothing more than a Liverpool on a steeplechase, no different than racing neck or nothing across the countryside, taking every stile and fence as they came—

never mind this horse wasn't a trained hunter, never mind he hadn't a clue what this horse possessed by way of skill.

The edge of the dock loomed. Brennan counted down the strides. *Four, three, two...* Brennan lifted his seat, his body balancing over the horse's neck, giving the horse the least of his weight to carry over the distance. *One...* The horse's hooves gave a mighty push off the dock and they were soaring, airborne over the expanse of dark water. Brennan kept his body still, his eyes forward, forcing his thoughts ahead to the landing, forcing them away from failure, away from falling. It was going to be close and that wasn't good enough. Close wouldn't help him or the horse.

Hooves hit wood. Brennan registered a moment's relief before the horse went down, the momentum of the landing taking the horse to its knees. The horse stumbled and fell on the deck of the boat. Everything was chaos. Hands were on him, Haviland pulling him free of the rolling animal, Archer and Nolan at the horse's head, urging it to stay down.

Down! He reached frantically for Haviland,

pushing him to the deck, and covering his friend with his body. The real danger wasn't the horse crushing anyone; it was the men on the dock with their pistols. They might have been far enough away from the dock to exceed a horse's jumping range, but not a pistol's. Haviland would not accidentally die for him because he'd been too lazy to roll out of a whore's bed on time. Brennan felt Haviland struggle to rise beneath him, motivated by instinctive curiosity, perhaps not fully understanding the gravity of the situation. 'Stay down!' Brennan shouted, his voice sharp as a bullet whined overhead.

Brennan made sure they stayed down a good long while until he felt certain the boat was out of range. He rose first. If anyone had to pay for his sins, it would be him alone. He looked about, giving the all-clear signal. His friends got to their feet, brushing off their clothes and exclaiming over his arrival.

Haviland dusted off his trousers, his gaze moving beyond Brennan's shoulder. Brennan turned his head, following Haviland's stare. He could see the men on the docks shaking impotent fists in their direction. Brennan flashed them an obscene gesture of confident victory. The greatcoat he'd been forced to leave behind settled any debt he had with Cynthia and her thugs. One button alone was worth the night.

'Good lord, Bren, what have you got yourself into now?' Haviland's voice was gruff with concern, not anger.

Brennan stopped in the midst of tucking in his shirt tails and quirked an auburn eyebrow at his friend in mock chagrin, trying to keep things light. 'Is that any way to greet the friend who just saved your life?' He didn't do well with any show of sincere emotion and Haviland was nothing if not sincere. It tore at him to see his friend worried and to know he was the cause of it. Again. This wouldn't be the first time.

Haviland answered with a raised dark brow of his own. '*My* life, is it? I rather thought it was yours.' He stepped forward and pulled Brennan into an embrace, pounding him on the back affectionately. 'I thought you were going to miss the boat, you stupid fool.'

Brennan returned the embrace for a moment, his voice low for Haviland alone. 'You told me all I had to do was show up and I did.'

Haviland laughed, which was what Brennan had intended. Haviland needed to laugh more. He was far too serious, especially these last three months. Brennan knew he'd been busy with arrangements for the trip, but Brennan thought the seriousness came from more than that, from something deeper. Although it was hard to imagine Haviland with any real problems. His life was perfect inside and out.

If there was trouble inside Haviland's life, Brennan would know. He'd been going home with Haviland since he was fifteen and Haviland had taken pity on him in school. Haviland's family was always appropriately civil, always politely welcoming, their home always well ordered, his mother at one end of the dinner table smiling at his father at the other end. It made his own home look like absolute chaos. Even his farewell had been devoid of any real feeling. There'd been no organised goodbye dinner, no teary farewells in the hallway the day he'd left, much as he imagined there'd been at Haviland's town house.

His own father had called him into the study five minutes before his scheduled departure, barely enough time to share a final drink. It wasn't even a private moment. Nolan had been with him, having come to collect him. His father's parting words to him in London had been, 'Don't get syphilis. You know...' He'd stammered it awkwardly, never comfortable with his paternal role. 'You know, just in case.' Brennan had heard the rest of that unspoken message: *just in case we need you, just in case your brother can't get the job done with that mousy Mathilda he married.* Then his father had pressed a package of French letters in his hand with a wink, 'the best they make'.

The comment had been entirely at odds with his father's attempt at preaching sexual responsibility. Then again, perhaps not so incongruous. His father had always been more interested in being his friend than a paternal head of the house when he was interested at all. As farewells went, it was what Brennan had expected. It just wasn't what he had hoped. After all, he'd be gone at least a year, perhaps longer. As last words and moments went, Brennan would have preferred *'I love you, I will miss you, be safe'*.

Perhaps Nolan was right. Nolan had hypothesised late one very drunk night that he sought out sex to fill an emotional gap in his life. Nolan prided himself on being a student of human nature. At the time, Brennan had laughed. It was easier to laugh at such ideas than admit to them. No one liked acknowledging deficiencies.

Archer led the horse away to a makeshift stall and the three of them took up positions at the rail, Nolan on one side of him, Haviland on the other as England grew tiny in the distance. Nolan shot him a side glance, mischief quirking his mouth into a half grin. 'So,' Nolan drawled, 'the real question isn't *where* you've been, but was she worth it?'

Brennan laughed, because it was indeed hard to admit to mistakes, especially one's own. 'Always, Nol, always.' He silently toasted a fading England. Here was to one more escape.

Chapter Two

Kardamyli, on the Greek Peloponnesian
Peninsula—early spring, 1837

He was going to need an escape plan. Again.
The party in the town square to celebrate Konstantine's birthday was only an hour in and
Brennan was already headed for disaster of
the female sort, careening towards it actually.
He should not have danced with Katerina Stefanos. Now, he was trapped with her on one
side of him, her father on the other, espousing
his daughter's wifely merits to the group, but
especially to him.

Somehow, Brennan had thought this time
it would be different. He always thought that,
but this time he'd really believed it because

this time *he* was different or at least he'd thought so. He'd reached the ends of Europe here on the southernmost tip of the Peloponnesian Peninsula, he'd swapped his trousers for the traditional *foustanella*—the kilt worn by men in Greece. He'd traded in the traditional sights that populated an Englishman's Grand Tour—the Acropolis with its Parthenon, Olympia with its pillared ruins—for the remote fishing village of Kardamyli, a town that was barely on the map, let alone the Grand Tour. In short, he had gone native, as far as an auburn-haired Englishman on the Greek peninsula could go, both figuratively and geographically.

And it hadn't mattered. Not really. It went to prove that you could take the boy out of trouble, but you couldn't take trouble out of the boy. For all the outward changes he'd wrought, for the thousand miles he had travelled, there were, apparently, some things he had not succeeded in outrunning, mainly his penchant for landing in compromising situations without truly meaning to. There'd been the woman in Dover before he'd sailed, the rather possessive prostitute in Paris, the Alpine beauty in Bern, the opera singer in Venice *and* the opera singer in Milan because he hadn't learned his lesson the first time. The list was rather, um, lengthy. Now, there was Katerina Stefanos to add to it, another woman who didn't understand he wasn't looking to make a commitment, wasn't *capable* of making one.

Her thickset father slapped a paternal hand on his shoulder, his voice booming out to the group over the music. 'My Katerina makes the best *diples* in the village. A man will never go hungry with such a woman as her for his wife. A fine cook she is and a fine housekeeper, too, her linens are the whitest, her stitches the straightest. Her mother has taught her well and she has…'

Wait for it. Brennan fought the urge to cringe. He knew what was coming next, testimony to how many times he'd heard it in the last month: *two olive groves as her dowry*. He knew! He knew! Enough already! Beside him, the lovely Katerina of the two olive groves tossed her dark hair and looped a bold, proprietary hand through his arm, further indication he had to move fast.

His sense of urgency was beginning to border on panic. Of all the situations he'd been in, this one was by far the most dangerous. None of the other women in his past had wanted to *marry* him. They weren't the marrying types. They'd merely wanted his patronage and his prick. Katerina and her father wanted something substantially more, ah, permanent. It might be time to start thinking of a more permanent solution on his end, too. Maybe this was a sign it was time to move on. He'd been here six months, longer than he'd stayed anywhere on his tour. Where he went from here wasn't important at the moment. He'd think about that later. Right now, he was interested in a more immediate solution and for that, he'd need an ally. This time, he didn't have his companions to extricate him. There was no Haviland, no Archer, no Nolan to help him out of this. He would have to manufacture an ally on his own.

Brennan scanned the perimeter of the dance area, looking for something—*someone*—that might give him a reason to gracefully leave the group. There was no question of leaving the party itself so soon. It was Konstantine's birthday and his friend had made a point of wanting him there. Brennan couldn't disappoint him with an early departure especially when everyone in the village was here.

'There is an old stone house on the far side of the olive groves. Father says it wouldn't take much to fix up.' Katerina beamed, her dark eyes slanting his way with a coy glance.

Olive groves and a house, could they make it any easier for him? Most men of the sort who populated this part of the world would have said yes ages ago. Brennan shifted uneasily on his feet. It was getting harder and harder to refuse politely without appearing rude, or crazy. What man turned down the offer of a pretty wife, a house and an income? No one. That was the problem. There was *no one*. The recent war had claimed the lives of over twenty thousand. Like many small villages on the peninsula, Kardamyli lacked a surplus of marriageable young men. On those grounds, Brennan understood the persistence of the

Stefanos. He even empathised with them. Who was there to marry these girls now with so many young men dead? But he could not *sympathise* with them…that was where he had to draw the line. Whomever Katerina Stefanos and her unmarried comrades-in-arms wed, it would not be him.

He should have seen it coming. Six months was a long time. He'd lived here, he'd spent his days in hard labour beside the men, heaving burgeoning nets of fish until his arms ached, or picking olives during the endless hours of the October harvest. He had revelled in the hard labour and the usefulness of his days. He'd been accepted as one of them with his *foustanella* and desire for hard work. The village had generously welcomed him and the women knew how to show their appreciation with delicious meals made up of exotically named foods: souvlakis, moussaka, spanakopita, spit-cooked lamb, the tzatziki and always the warm fresh-baked pita into which any number of fillings could be stuffed.

Only now, that generosity was changing. It had been evident long before Katerina had been so bold as to pull him into the birthday dancing. It had been there in the conversations with the men these past few weeks, a new undertone about his future in the village. Which of the girls did he fancy? Katerina with her olive groves or perhaps Maria, whose father would give a son-in-law half interest in his fishing boats?

There were so many pretty choices if marriage tempted him. It didn't and he'd chosen to ignore the signs, because of what they meant. He had two choices: settling down and marrying one of the village beauties, or leaving. He wasn't ready to leave Kardamyli. For the moment, there was no place he would rather be than here, in the town centre with its music and lanterns and plank tables groaning with food. No ballroom in London could look finer.

In spite of the new pressure to marry, he liked it here, better than London, better than anywhere he'd been in Europe over the last two years. There had to be middle ground somewhere between matrimony and moving on, some way to prove his loyalty to the village without marrying for it. There also had to be middle ground tonight, too, a place between rudely leaving the party to escape Katerina or staying at the price of pledging his eternal devotion. If he could only find it and fast.

Katerina discreetly brushed her breasts against his arm and her father gripped his shoulder in not-so-subtle encouragement that he declare himself. After all, Alexei Stefanos had put the world at his feet. What more could a father do for a beloved child? It was more than his father had ever done for him. But the only thought Brennan could muster was *run*!

Any moment Katerina was going to suggest they take a stroll and he definitely didn't want to do that. He had no doubt he'd come back compromised. Funny, he'd always thought if there was to be any compromising situations in his life, they would be the other way around. His panic was full-fledged now. *Run, run, run*, pounded in his head. To where? To whom?

Brennan could see Konstantine making the rounds, visiting each cluster of guests. He would reach their group shortly and Brennan knew a little relief. There would be some help in that, but he would need a plan in place by the time Kon got there.

Brennan quartered the agora with his eyes, his gaze taking in the dancers in the middle, the groups of partygoers on the perimeter, his eyes mentally assessing and discarding his options for an ally; no, not her—too desperate; no, too competitive; already married; good heavens, no, just no; maybe, no, no, no. Two-thirds of the way through the guests he stopped. This would never work. He was being too picky.

His gaze started around the perimeter once more. No, no, *wait*. His eyes drifted back to the shadows. There was someone standing on the edge of the light. He recognised her as Patra Tspiras, the widow who bought fish from Konstantine, and she was alone. Better yet. He wouldn't have to explain himself to everyone around her. Their eyes brushed for the briefest of moments. Her gaze slid away with a quickness that implied guilt over having been caught staring. A smile quirked at his lips. She'd been watching him. It was settled.

He would run to her. Escape was in sight. He just needed to pick his moment.

Konstantine approached the group, slapping guests on the back and kissing cheeks. 'Are we having fun?' he asked. His voice, loud like Stefanos's, boomed over the music to be heard. He gave a broad wink to everyone, making an expansive gesture with his hands. 'Tonight, I insist everyone have a good time. There is plenty to eat and to drink.'

Impromptu toasts to Konstantine's good health went up around them. Brennan saw his opening. He jerked his head towards the dark corner of the agora where Patra stood. 'I think you've succeeded, Kon, with all but one. Perhaps I should go and spread the party cheer.' He gave a farewell nod to the group and was off before anyone could protest, relief bringing a wide smile to his lips as he sought out the source of his liberation.

She did *not* want to be here! Patra covertly slipped a plate of baklava into the shadows, wishing she could disappear as easily. Well-meaning friends had been trying to feed her all night. They'd been trying to do more than feed her, in fact; they wanted her to eat, to dance, specifically they wanted her to dance with a sudden rash of male relatives, all of them of an older persuasion, who'd come from neighbouring villages. Patra wanted no part of it. She couldn't have any part of it even if she did desire one of them.

She would not have come at all if she could have managed it, but it would have been far harder to explain why she hadn't come than to simply come and sneak off later once the niceties had been observed. In compromise, she stood off to the side of the festivities, trying hard to blend into the dark and thankful for the small miracle that for a few moments she was alone.

She was grateful for her friends, but tonight she had little tolerance for their new and misdirected efforts. The older women who had surrounded her in the years since her husband's death had decided amongst themselves she had mourned Dimitri long enough. It was time for her to remarry, no matter how many times she told them she had no intentions of marrying again.

A loud burst of laughter from the dancing drew her eye to its source, coaxing a small smile from her. Of course. She shouldn't be surprised the laughter belonged to the Englishman, Brennan Carr, who was twirling Katerina Stefanos through the steps of a dance. They made an attractive couple with their vivacious smiles and striking good looks.

Patra felt a twinge of general envy watching them, or was that wistfulness? She and Dimitri had been that way; every day, every dance, every night, a chance to celebrate their life together. Now, that life was over, one more casualty in the fight for an independent Greece, a fight that had taken her husband and her *naïveté* with it. The naïve loved wholly, completely with mind, body and soul. She never wanted to risk feeling that way again. It took too much from a person, made oneself too vulnerable. But there were plenty of green girls in the village who were willing to risk it. She was probably the only woman in Kardamyli between sixteen and sixty who didn't entertain 'interest of a more personal nature' in Brennan Carr. Then again, she was the only one who couldn't risk it.

The dance ended and she watched Brennan lead Katerina back to her father. The look on Katerina's face was happily possessive. Patra wondered if the Englishman understood. She might hover on the periphery of village life, but even she knew the fathers of Kardamyli were angling to make Brennan a more permanent member of the community.

Patra watched Brennan shift uneasily on his feet, his eyes darting through the crowd, looking for something, someone. Ah, so he *did* know. He was getting nervous, as well he should. The sort of Englishman who would come to Kardamyli was not the sort who would stay. Brennan Carr was an adventurer. Marriage and a wife would put a stop to those adventures.

He was quartering the crowd with his eyes, his gaze inevitably headed her way. She should step, out of his path. She didn't want company and yet something stubborn encouraged her eyes to meet his when they passed, encouraged her gaze to linger on his in a brief connection before she understood what it was asking. He was looking for an escape and he had settled on her. She moved her gaze away and stepped back, but the damage was done. It was too late to second-guess her choice. She'd stared too long. Now, Brennan Carr was headed her direction, all blue eyes and swagger, and there was no one to blame but herself.

People would be bound to notice, in part because this was most uncharacteristic of her, but mostly because of *him*. It was no secret among the women folk he'd been setting hearts astir since his arrival. But she'd prudently kept her distance for many reasons. She simply wasn't interested and even if she was, he was in his late twenties and far too young for her mature thirty-five, until, quite obviously, now.

Patra swallowed. He stood in front of her, his eyes as blue as gossip reported, his strong tan hands hitched in the wide leather belt of his *foustanella* riding low on his hips, as he drawled with all the cocky confidence of a man who knew he was right, '*You* were watching me.'

'I was *concerned* for you,' Patra corrected, meeting his boldness with a coolness of her own. She nodded in the direction of the Stefanos. 'You didn't look entirely comfortable with the proceedings.'

'As well I wasn't.' His grin broadened and her breath caught. He had a most expressive face when he smiled. The bones were magnificent, a sculptor's dream: sharp, jutting cheekbones that framed the straight length of his nose and a mouth that promised to deliver all nature of sin. Objectively speaking, Patra could see what all the fuss was about and what all the fuss was *going* to be about if he stayed around much longer. Women would go to war over a man like him. He'd become their very own version of a Helen.

He gave her a meaningful look, his eyes skimming her mouth. His voice dropped to a most private level as his body angled close to hers so that his quiet words could be heard above the music without calling public attention to them. 'You have rescued me. I am prepared to be grateful.'

Dear lord, he was audacious! His words sent a bolt of unlooked-for white heat straight through her, whether she was interested or not. A woman might have survived him if all he possessed was a pretty face, but he had charm, too, loads of it, and there were those eyes to consider; a shockingly dark blue like the Mediterranean at sunset. She'd already felt the power of them when he'd sought her out, and now she felt it again, more intensely, as those eyes bestowed the briefest of glances on her lips.

An unwary woman would be easily seduced. But she had left her *naïveté* behind years ago. She was no Katerina Stefanos, or Maria Kouplos, whose heads were filled with idealistic visions of love and marriage. And yet she was not immune to the heat of his body, the smell of his clean, simple soap or those long, strong legs of his, bare and tan in his *foustanella*.

In response, a little daring of her own arose. He'd come to her needing a distraction, an escape, from husband-seeking fathers. She could give him that. In exchange for sanctuary, maybe he could give her a little escape, too—an escape from the ill-fated matchmaking efforts of the village matriarchs. Why not let him be grateful? Judiciously grateful, of course. She wasn't about to go slinking off with him into dark corners for even darker kisses.

Patra cocked her head and gave him a coy smile that was perhaps out of practice. 'Grateful? Are your favours so easily distributed, then?' He could be grateful, but she wouldn't make it easy on him. He had a small test to pass first. 'Do you even know my name?' She had her pride. He might stoke her curiosity, but not enough for her to settle for being nothing more than an interchangeable part in his scheme to resist Katerina's plans.

His blue eyes glinted with mischievous satisfaction as he rose to the challenge. 'Patra Tspiras,' he announced. 'I've seen you in the village, at the market. You buy Konstantine's fish on Wednesdays.'

Patra was glad for the darkness. She could

feel a flattered blush start, hot on her cheeks. He'd noticed her. He'd asked about her. The idea that she found pleasure in knowing he'd sought out that tiny piece of information about her was a silly, girlish reaction.

It was the way he smiled when he said it that made it seem personal, important. It was how he said it, too. Together, it was a most potent combination that did all sorts of things to her pulse against her will. It reminded her she was Patra Tspiras, not simply Dimitri's widow, as if her marriage and her husband were all that defined her person. She would always be Dimitri's widow, it was part of who she'd become but not the sum. Sometimes she wanted only to be Patra, to simply belong to herself, to her wants and desires instead of what others required of her whether they knew it or not.

He made a small bow, his hand on his chest. 'I'm Brennan Carr.'

She cut him off with a laugh. 'I know. Everyone knows.'

He laughed, too, grinning as he offered his arm. 'In that case, introductions are concluded. I promised Konstantine I would see to your cheer. Would you do me the honour of a dance?' He leaned in close once more and she caught the scent of his soap. 'I think it would ensure the authenticity of my escape, don't you?'

And hers, too, Patra thought, taking his arm, even if he was unaware of the favor he did her. For a few minutes she would make her wish come true. For a few minutes, she would simply be Patra. Surely there was no harm in that.

Chapter Three

Safe was the first word that sprang to mind as Brennan manoeuvred them on to the crowded dance floor. Patra Tsipiras was *safe*. She expected nothing from him beyond the moment because she, too, had been looking for an escape. He'd seen it in her eyes when their gazes had brushed. They took up their positions. He fitted his hand to her waist. She placed hers on his upper arm and Brennan leaned in, breathing the comforting scents of lavender and sage. He flashed her a cheeky grin. 'Be warned, I mean to change your mind.'

'About what?' She laughed up at him, her dark eyes sparking as they considered him, and Brennan had the distinct impression she was flirting, a realisation that took him somewhat by surprise. She was a sober sort in the market. He couldn't recall ever having seen her smile.

The music began and Brennan took them into the first steps of a fast country gallop, his eyes never leaving hers. He might have been unprepared for her bold response, but by Jove he would answer it with boldness of his own. He called her out with a friendly wink and a smile. '*You* don't want to be here.'

She blushed at the truth, but her gaze held as he took them through a fast turn. 'Was it that obvious?' She laughed again, this time a little breathless, her hair starting to fall in a becoming caramel spill that softened the angles of her face.

Brennan's smile broadened. 'Not as obvious as shoving baklava under a bush.'

'Oh, no, you saw!' She groaned with good humour.

'Don't you like baklava?' Brennan joked.

'Not three plates of it.' She laughed again and he swung her through a turn that left her gasping. If there was one thing he was good at, it was dancing. Actually, there were two things he was good at. One usually led to the other, although it wouldn't tonight. Patra Tsipiras was safe, he reminded himself. She was a quiet widow devoted to her late husband's memory. But he was having a hard time reconciling what he knew to the woman in his arms.

There was nothing quiet about this woman, everything about her was alive—her eyes, her body, her throaty laughter—and it spurred him on. He took the turns hard to feel her body come against his, he cut a sharp pattern through the centre of the dancers, dragging her close to do it and she matched him step for step, a live, burning, *beautiful* flame.

How had he not noticed before, all those days in the fish market? How had he not seen the dark fire of her eyes? Not heard the innate sensuality of her laugh? Not *felt* the thrum of life that emanated from her? Probably because he hadn't been looking and she hadn't made it easy. There'd been no reason for either of them to have done otherwise. But tonight was different. Tonight, they needed each other.

The dance ended, the musicians flowing into a reel he loved. Patra turned to go. He saw her hesitate when he made no move to escort her from the floor. Brennan closed a hand about her wrist, his voice low and insistent. 'One more dance, Patra. Please.' He didn't wait for an answer, merely moved them into position and let her happen to him all over again.

'We'd better stop at two,' Patra suggested, breathing hard at the end of the reel, the voice of wisdom when he would have stayed on the floor with her. This wasn't London, after all, and there was no hard-and-fast rule about a two-dance limit. 'I think we can safely assume you've satisfied authenticity's needs.'

Probably more than satisfied it. He might have exceeded it, if the looks Katerina Stefanos was directing his way were any indicator. Patra noticed it. 'Katerina doesn't look pleased. Perhaps you'd better go back and reassure her of your affections.'

Brennan shook his head, adrenaline still fuelling him. 'How could I do that when you've asked me to escort you home?' It was a bold gambit. They had not spoken of such plans. Would she refuse? Would she think leaving with him stirred a larger scandal than staying? But she was caught up in the euphoria of the dance, too.

'Oh, I have, have I?'

Brennan pulled a mockingly serious face. 'You have, most definitely. There's a rock in your shoe that is wreaking havoc with your foot.'

She arched incredulous dark brows. 'A rock? How about we settle for a pebble?' Then she added with a sly smile, 'for authenticity's sake of course.'

For her part, Patra did a credible job manufacturing a slight limp while Brennan made their excuses to Konstantine. They were under way within minutes. There was no drama in slipping off, no covertly delivered messages with complicated instructions for a private meeting. He'd simply left with her.

Safe was turning into *fun*. So much fun, in fact, Brennan was in no hurry to see the evening end. Who would have thought the small event of strolling down a dirt road, Patra's arm tucked loosely through his, could be so enjoyable? Overhead the stars were out, even brighter now that they were away from the party lights. Brennan knew exactly where he wanted to go. They'd reached a fork in the path, the left leading up a hill towards one of his favourite places. The right led to her home, although he'd never been there. It was something everyone in a small town knew. Everyone knew where everyone lived. If he took her there, it would lead to the end of the evening. Patra turned to the right. He made no attempt to follow her or to release her arm. It was decision time.

She tossed him a quizzical look, her eyes dropping to the light grip he had on her arm. 'I can see myself on from here.'

'Do you want to go home?' Brennan let his eyes scan her face, let them linger on her eyes, looking for truth. He held up his other hand, revealing the prize he carried. He had grabbed it off a table as they'd left the party. 'I've got a bottle of wine and the view at the top of the hill is spectacular.' He grinned. 'So, let me ask you again. Do you really want to go home?'

The question wasn't meant to be difficult. She *should* want that, just as Patra knew what the right answer was: yes. She wanted to go home, wanted to be alone. That had been her original intent. She'd fulfilled her end of the bargain. She'd rescued him from Katerina's possessive clutches. She had every right to claim her escape, and yet, that smile of his and those eyes on her face were the undoing of her. She wasn't naïve. She knew what he wanted, what all young men wanted. She'd be a liar if she didn't admit to being at least a little flattered he wanted some of her attention. She'd be a liar, too, if she didn't admit her attraction to him. It was hard to be alone even when there was no other choice and she'd been alone so very long. She'd been good for oh, so very long, too—not calling attention to herself, living quietly on the edges of society in all ways, encouraging no one to take an interest in her. Now, here *he* was; tempting her with his good looks and his superb dancing. He tempted her with more than that. He was fun and he was kind. Those qualities were far more important than looks, she'd learned. Looks could be deceiving. Actions less so. She'd noticed tonight how he'd not wanted to embarrass Katerina and he would not force his attentions where they were not wanted. He was giving her the choice to climb the hill.

Or not. If she said no, he'd escort her home, wine unopened, view unseen. Kisses untasted, bodies untried. The last part rose unbidden in her mind. He might be willing to push those boundaries, but she was not. If she went up that hill, she needed some rules in place with herself. She was *not* kissing this bold English adventurer who had probably kissed half of Europe on his journey here. All right, *no* kissing. Other than that, why not? Why not climb that hill and look at the stars. Temptation beckoned. Surely one night would be safe enough. Who would know? Who would tell? And the Englishman wouldn't be here for ever. If the matchmakers in the village didn't take care of that, his own nature would. He was perfectly safe as long as it was just one night.

Patra cocked her head to one side, giving the impression of serious consideration. 'You said you have wine?'

Brennan shook the bottle. 'Are you in?' He held out his hand. 'Come on. It will be worth it, I promise.'

* * *

It had better be, Patra groused halfway up. The hill was steeper than she'd anticipated and dancing shoes weren't ideal for climbing in the dark. If she hadn't had a real pebble in her shoe when they'd left the dance, she most likely did now. Brennan reached out a hand for her and she gladly took it.

'How are you doing? We're almost there.' She could hear the smile in his words, feel his enthusiasm, as he offered her encouragement. It struck her then that Brennan Carr was a little bit impetuous. People didn't simply, spontaneously, climb hills in the dark. No, he wasn't just a 'little bit' impetuous. She'd wager he was *a lot* impetuous. If he lived like he danced, he was probably in the habit of throwing himself headlong into adventure after adventure without thinking about the consequences until it was too late, like he had with Katerina Stefanos. What had started out as fun had quickly turned into something more serious.

Oh, this was bad, she didn't want to be curious about him. Curiosity led to questions and questions led to answers and answers to familiarity. The less she knew about him, the better for them both.

The ground smoothed out and the shrubbery gave way, the path expanding to a wide, flat area. Brennan gave an exultant crow, 'We made it! Just look at that!'

She had to concede the view *was* spectacular, well worth every pebble in her shoes. The sky seemed close enough to touch, the stars near enough to pluck with her fingers, while down below, she could make out the dark shape of boats bobbing in the harbour and the faint glow from Konstantine's party. Down there, the crowd would be noisy, but up here, it was quiet and peaceful. There was no music other than the crickets and the night birds. Behind her, she could hear Brennan rustling in the bushes.

'Here it is,' he announced, pulling out a blanket. He shook it free of little pieces of twigs and dried leaves before spreading it on the hill. He patted the spot beside him. 'Come and sit, Patra, and enjoy our view.'

She sat and he worked the cork loose on the bottle, pulling it the last bit of the way with his teeth. 'I don't suppose you have any glasses under a bush, too?' she teased.

He gave a perplexed glance. 'No, why would I?'

Patra shrugged, feeling silly for having asked. 'I just thought, since you were so prepared...'

He grinned, unfazed by her implication. 'I come up here almost every night to watch the sunset and sometimes to think.' He jostled her with a friendly elbow. 'You're surprised. You thought I brought girls up here all the time.' He passed her the bottle, letting her drink first. 'You're the only one and I wasn't even sure you would come. It seemed presumptuous of me to bring glasses.'

'Maybe you say that to all the girls,' she pressed, testing only partly in jest. There wasn't a girl in the village who wouldn't climb this hill with him.

'Well, I don't.' Brennan gave her a firm look. 'You'll just have to trust me.' She'd like to, Patra realised. She supposed it was the inviting openness of his face. Women probably confided in him all the time. It had been a long time since she'd trusted anyone, confided in anyone. Her secrets were too dark for that. There was no one she could tell, no one she could burden with the evil that hovered on the fringes of her life. But hope hovered on those fringes, too. Maybe the evil was gone now. It had been four years since Castor Apollonius had last pressed his wicked suit. Perhaps this time he was gone for good, finally convinced she would never be his. Maybe, she could risk just a little.

'Can you do without them? The glasses?' Brennan asked.

During the war, she'd done without a lot more than glasses. Patra shot him a daring look and tipped the bottle back, taking a deep swallow of the rich red wine, feeling adventurous and decadent—for a moment, free. The wine tasted good after the dancing and the climbing. She passed the bottle back, watching him drink deeply and run his sleeve around the rim before giving it back.

Brennan stretched out, propping his head on one arm as he pointed to the sky. 'Tell me what you know about the stars. There's Cassiopeia, there's Orion's Belt.' He gestured to the familiar arrangements.

'There's Gemini, the twins, there's Draco,' Patra added, scanning the sky. It was better to focus on the stars than to think too much about the very masculine body stretched out beside her in a pose of rather shocking familiarity, as if they were old friends or something more, two people used to one another's bodies instead of strangers who had shared a dance and an escape. But he was not at all concerned about the intimacy of his pose or their proximity to one another.

'You know a lot of them. I'm impressed.' Brennan's gaze shifted from the stars to her and she met his eyes, a most dangerous challenge.

'When you grow up around boats and sailors you learn the stars early. Can't afford not to.' She reached for the bottle.

'Have you lived here all your life?' Brennan's tone was soft, his fingers gentle as they closed around hers, taking back the bottle.

'All of my married life. Kardamyli is my husband's home. I came here as his bride.' As an innocent eighteen-year-old, flushed with love, looking forward to the life she and Dimitri would make in his town. She did not volunteer where she was from. It would make for more questions. Did she miss her home? Did she ever think of going back there? Did she have family? Those answers dug up memories she didn't want tonight, reminders of all she'd lost instead of focusing on all that she still had. 'What about you? Where do you live?' Perhaps if he talked about himself, he'd be less inclined to want to talk about her.

'I'm from a place called Sussex, south-east of London.' He seemed reluctant to say more. She understood. Places carried memories. She hadn't meant to pry, only to distract. 'I'm sorry, you don't like to talk about it.'

Brennan shook his head. 'No, it's just that I've been gone for two years. It doesn't seem like I'm from there any more. I've been travelling with friends. We've seen a lot of places and now I suppose I feel a little rootless.'

She'd not heard of the friends before. 'Where are your friends now? Will they be joining you?'

'No.' Brennan chuckled, his eyes starting to spark again. 'The funny thing is, they all got married. Haviland married in Paris, Archer in Siena and Nolan in Verona, although Nolan met his bride in Venice. They all asked me to stay with them, but I just wanted to keep moving.'

Patra played with the fringe of the blanket, twisting it between her fingers, daring herself to ask more personal questions, daring herself to satisfy her selfish curiosity. 'So here you are. Kardamyli isn't exactly a tourist destination.'

Brennan shrugged again, unbothered by her probing. How wonderful to be such an open book. 'I like it here, though. I like being some place where there's no other Englishmen, no one who might know me. Here, I can just be me.' He let out a sound that was half groan, half laugh as if he was remembering something unpleasant. 'You should have seen Rome. It was crawling with English. I could go days without seeing any Italians. It was awful.'

She laughed with him because his laughter was infectious and his stories heartfelt. One couldn't help but be taken in by his sincerity. He was different than her, his *life* was different. He'd seen so much of the world while she had seen Kardamyli and the town she'd been born in. To her, the fifteen-mile journey between her town and Dimitri's had been significant, important.

He gave her a lopsided grin. 'If I wanted to see Englishmen, I would have stayed home.'

'I wouldn't know, I haven't been more than twenty miles from here my entire life,' Patra said softly. The disparity in their ages seemed to flip. She was thirty-five and yet, in some ways, she lacked his worldly experiences.

He considered her for a long moment, his eyes quieting, his gaze turning serious. His smile faded to be replaced by a small, almost rueful grin. His hand came up to stroke her hair, to cup her cheek. All she had to do was turn her head and kiss his palm. That was the wine talking. The bottle was nearly empty now and she knew she'd been responsible for a significant portion of it. If she kissed his palm, it would invite other kisses, kisses she'd promised herself to avoid.

His voice was soft when he spoke, too. 'That's a good sign. You mustn't have anything to run from.'

How she wanted to argue! It wasn't true. She had plenty to run from: memories of Dimitri, memories of the war, memories of the man who'd led Dimitri and other patriots to their deaths, who'd coaxed her into believing such sacrifice was worth it. But to argue would mean she'd have to prove it, she'd have to tell her stories, to expose herself.

Brennan tugged at her hand. 'Come…lie down, Patra.' And she did, because it was the lesser of two evils to lie down beside him and stare at the skies than to let the evening be overrun with memories of things she couldn't change and people she couldn't save.

'What do you have to run from?' She stretched out beside him, matching his pose, her head resting on her hand. She had not been this close to a man in ages, certainly not such a virile one.

'Everything. Nothing.' His blue eyes flirted with her quietly, the night and the stars adding their own layers of intimacy to this impetuous wine picnic. He would be intoxicating even without the drink. She had to be careful. She hadn't broken her rule…yet, but she was dancing close to the fire. She was recognising in hindsight there were probably other promises she should have made herself. *Don't lie down with a man you don't know, don't stare at the stars with him and absolutely don't drink wine with him.*

'There was no reason to stay in England, or Paris, or Venice, or Milan, or Siena.' Brennan's hand stroked her hair, pushing a strand behind her ear. It was becoming far too easy to let him touch her. It felt far too good.

'And Kardamyli?' The words were out of her mouth before she could think better of them. Reasons to stay were dangerous.

'We'll see. I like it here.' The implied *but* hovered in the air. Oh, he was smooth, he knew all the right things to say: *If a woman would give me a reason to stay, I might consider it.* No wonder Katerina Stefanos had fallen for him. He could certainly bait a hook.

She decided to give him a dose of reality, and perhaps a dose for herself, too—a reminder that he was not for her…that she was merely looking for an escape from her friends' well-meaning efforts. 'There may be conditions placed on your ability to stay.' *Like taking a wife.*

He merely gave one his shrugs, unconcerned about future consequences. 'You've managed to remain unattached. I am sure I will, too. Maybe that's something we could work on together.' His hand drifted to the back of her neck, fingers tangling in her hair, cradling it as he had done her cheek. His eyes dropped to her lips, his head angled slowly in fair warning, giving her time to choose her response and then he made his move, closing the gap between them with swift confidence, his mouth moving fast and sure over hers.

Chapter Four

She let him. She wasn't technically breaking her promise. *He* was kissing *her*, after all, and she couldn't very well control *his* actions. It was a hastily done rationalisation, one she was probably going to regret…later. Right now, her lips, her body were too busy sinking into his to regret much of anything.

Good lord, he could kiss. His mouth was patient, savouring hers, seducing hers with its slow confidence. He was not in doubt about the conclusion of the interlude and in no hurry to get there. His tongue made a languorous perusal of her mouth, his hands running up her back, drawing her close to him on the blanket. Oh, how she wanted to be close, to feel the heat of him, the muscled press of his body.

Shc had not realised how hungry she was for such contact and it had to stop. This could not happen, no matter how enjoyable. If he wasn't able to see the ramifications of this, she would, for both of them. The village wouldn't tolerate it, not when he'd been flirting with the eligible girls and doing heaven knew what else with them. Her pride would not stand it either. He couldn't use her like this and then leave her. There were other reasons, too, but these were the most immediate.

Brennan's hand was warm at her leg, sliding beneath her skirt, resting on her knee. She pushed gently at his chest and pulled away with a shake of her head. His blue eyes reflected his puzzlement, his disappointment. She tried to soften her words with a smile, but her voice was stern, leaving no quarter for argument. 'I think it's time to go home.'

'Really?' He wasn't going to give up easily. His auburn hair, tousled from her fingers, and the smoulder of those blue eyes were nearly irresistible as he formed his one-word rebuttal, challenging her suggestion.

Distance. She needed distance. Patra stumbled to her feet. If she stayed on the blanket a moment longer, he would win. He had too many advantages on his side and she could not allow that. His victory would be expensive for them both. Patra smoothed her skirts and began to re-pin her hair. 'Yes, *really*. It's late and we don't want to do this, not truly. In the morning, we'll regret it.' Her argument sounded clichéd and her hands shook as she re-pinned her hair.

He stood and moved into her, covering her hands with his. 'Let me.' He took the pins and deftly shoved them into her hair until it somewhat resembled its original self. He stared at her for a long moment, so close she could see the black flecks of his eyes amid the blue. A slow smile spread across his face. 'You'll do.' He leaned close, his voice conspiratorially low. 'I don't think anyone will guess you've been kissing that rake of an Englishman.'

He turned away and began to roll up the blanket, leaving no evidence of their presence. There had been self-derision mixed with the teasing lilt of his voice. It was hard to know how to take that remark. She'd accidentally hurt his feelings. 'I didn't do it only for me.' She felt compelled to defend herself. 'I did it for you, too. A scandal is the quickest way out of town or to the altar for you and it seemed to me that you weren't ready for either just yet.'

Brennan faced her, hands on hips, having put the blanket away under its bush. 'I don't need you to decide for me. *I* seldom regret anything in the mornings.'

The innuendo that *she* would not regret anything either had they carried their evening to a particular conclusion brought heat to her cheeks. In terms of personal satisfaction, he was most likely right. His dancing, his kissing, had served as very compelling references for his skills elsewhere. But it was the social aspect she was thinking of. Still, he was a young man and his pride in a sensitive area had been hurt.

Patra stepped forward, wanting to put a consoling hand on his arm, wanting to explain. 'Brennan, it's not that.' What did she say next? *It's not that I don't think you'd be fabulous in bed. From a purely technical standpoint, you would be phenomenal, I'm sure...* She could definitely *not* say that. She opted for something more platonic. 'There are many young women in the village who would welcome your attentions, but I am not one of them.'

Brennan crossed his arms and arched an auburn brow. 'Is that because you prefer the attentions of the grey-bearded men that buzz around you like so many bees to honey?' His tone was blunt and rough, at odds with his earlier smoothness. He was still smarting.

'What I prefer is my business.' She moved to head down the hill. It was past time to go. She had secrets to protect. By protecting them, she was protecting him even if he couldn't know or appreciate her efforts. She'd walk home alone if she had to. But Brennan was beside her, a hand at her elbow to help her navigate in the star-spiked darkness despite the tension rising between them. It proved again her earlier intuition that he was kind. Even in the midst of conflict, he remembered his word. Kind he might be, but he wasn't ready to leave the unpleasantness behind them on the hill.

'It's why you needed me tonight.' Brennan helped her over a rocky gap in the trail. 'You were looking to escape them.' He was far too perceptive. It would have been easier if he'd simply been a smooth-talking rake, but it appeared he was a bit more than that and it made him trickier to manage.

'My friends believe it's time for me to marry again, that I've mourned my husband long enough. I tell them I don't plan to wed, but they do not listen.' They didn't listen because they didn't understand the real reasons behind her resistance and she could not tell them.

'Instead, they have pooled their resources and brought to town any eligible relative they can lay their hands on.' Brennan chuckled as he summed up her predicament, the tension easing between them. Some of the teasing spark returned to the conversation. 'Is it that you're opposed to marrying again, or just opposed to marrying a greybeard?'

'Both.' They had to go slowly down the hill to avoid slipping on loose pebbles and she was too grateful for the support of his hand, steady and firm as he guided her down, to pull away. She envied him his confidence. He was in his prime and full of himself in all the best ways. How long would this strapping young man remain unchallenged, unmarked by the world? There was something appealing in the knowledge he'd never met a trial to which he was not equal.

'Why?' He persisted with a flirty wink. 'What if the right man came along, a younger man skilled with women?' He placed his hands at her waist and swung her over a small hole in the path. They were nearly at the bottom. Perhaps there would be less reason to touch her then, fewer reminders of what she'd given up on the hill, fewer reminders that *he* was a younger man with some skill with women.

'Marriage takes a lot out of a person, it requires an investment that exceeds anything you've ever known and then when you lose it, well, that takes even more from you. I simply don't think I'm up to it one more time.' She meant the words to be harsh, sobering, but they didn't have the desired effect.

He cocked his brow, *again*, and stopped long enough to study her, *again*. She was getting used to that look. 'Really?' She was getting used to that rebuttal, too. 'I didn't figure you for a quitter.'

Quitter? He thought *she* was a *quitter*? If there was one word to raise her ire, that was it. To hear it from someone who didn't know her, from an Englishman who hadn't even been here the last twelve years, bordered on insulting. 'You are out of line, Mr Carr. You have no idea what I've endured. Just because there is a cliff doesn't mean I have to jump off it.' She pushed past him—this was as good of an excuse as any to part ways before they reached her home. 'I can take it from here, Mr Carr. Thank you for the escort.'

Brennan's hand closed about her arm as she passed. 'The thing about cliffs, Patra, is that if you don't jump, you miss the chance to fly.' He did not let go. 'I promised to see you home and I will.' She could tell from the firmness of his grip there would be no shaking his resolve now.

They followed a bend in the road, the standard stucco-box shape of a Greek home coming into view beneath the moon and Patra braced herself for the embarrassment. It had never been a large home, but it had once been more neatly kept. Now, there was simply too much work to keep up on by herself and she dared not ask for help.

'Here we are.' She could hear the veiled disappointment in his tone. He'd expected something better from her than this ramshackle holding.

She nodded, seeing the place through Brennan's eyes. Even the moonlight couldn't soften the ragged edges of her once-proud house. The stucco needed a coat of whitewash, the shutters needed paint, the patio needed weeding, the grounds needed tending. The list was exhausting. All of her time was spent doing the most essential tasks, the ones that kept her fed and clothed. He would see the house and he would be glad she'd stopped things on the hill. He'd know the truth of her. She was the most pathetic of individuals; not just a widow, but a poor one with no family, a woman entirely alone in ways he couldn't begin to imagine.

His eyes moved over the house, but to his credit his gaze gave nothing away, and neither did his words. Patra felt a rush of gratitude for his discretion. 'Thank you,' she offered, leaving it open as to what she was thanking him for; he could choose to read it as he liked: the dance, the wine, the walk, the escort, for not commenting on her home. She'd not realised there was so much to thank him for.

Brennan put a restraining hand on her arm. 'Perhaps I should go in and make sure all is well.' He stepped forward, putting her behind him and drawing a short dagger from his belt. It was his way of registering there were no servants, no hired help minding the house while she was out.

'That's not necessary, I've never had any trouble,' Patra put in swiftly. The last thing she wanted was the charismatic personality and the hard, potent body of Brennan Carr filling up the tiny space of her home. She didn't trust herself to not change her mind about what she'd already rejected this evening.

He seemed to debate the wisdom of this decision with himself before relenting and sliding his dagger back into its sheath. 'If you're sure?'

'I am sure.' She smiled to persuade him. 'I

have a pistol and a dagger and I'm more than capable of using them.'

He gave her one of his disarming grins. 'I'm sure you can. The point is that you shouldn't have to. I'll wait until I see you light a lantern.' He let her walk away before his words brought her to a halt. 'Patra, I lied earlier. I'm regretting leaving you already.'

It was a sweet thing to say, just the right note to end the evening on, a note that recalled the intoxicating energy of the dancing and the rather heated energy of their kiss. A woman of less fortitude would have turned back. But Patra kept walking. She could not afford to give him an inch. She let her words float back to him as she stepped inside. 'Goodnight, Brennan.'

Brennan waited until he saw the light flare in the window, another idea flaring as he walked away. He'd deduced correctly she would not want his pity. She had her pride as much as any man. She might not *want* help, but she needed it. He understood now why she'd been so insistent on seeing herself home after a point. She'd requested twice that she go on alone. Did she think he would judge her? Did she think he hadn't been here on the peninsula long enough to appreciate the rugged nature of life beneath the hot sun and the toll it took? She would be wrong on both of those accounts. His own home wasn't much better, only larger.

She *needed* him whether she wanted to admit it or not and he needed her. He'd not been entirely joking up on the hill. Why not form an alliance? After seeing her home, there was even more reason for it. He was handy with tools and repairs. He'd done enough of them on his family's home, his father too distracted to see to the hiring of that work himself. Brennan would gladly trade his services for hers. If they could convince the village he was genuinely interested in her, even sincerely courting her, it would save them both the hassle of fending off unwanted suitors. Then, at the last moment, whenever that was, six more months from now, a year from now, a few weeks from now, he'd cry off, claiming an emergency that required his attentions in England.

The village could rage at him, could support her in her sorrow over being deserted. They'd vilify him for using one of their own so poorly, but he'd be too many miles away to care. It seemed like an ideal solution. Tonight, with Katerina Stefano's hand on his arm, he'd felt pressured to leave Kardamyli, but he wasn't ready to go, not just yet.

Brennan began to whistle in the night. Things were definitely starting to look up. Now, he just had to convince Patra of that. If it was true the way to a man's heart was through his stomach, it was also true that the way to a woman's heart was through a hammer. He had yet to meet a woman who could resist a man who provided for her needs in bed and out. Patra might have resisted him tonight, but that was just the beginning. She had yet to see Brennan Carr unleashed. This was turning out to be a challenge he was going to enjoy. After all, he didn't want to win her heart, just her compliance and he knew just how to do it.

Chapter Five

Ow! Bright light. Loud noise. Double ow! What was that pounding? Patra groaned and pulled a pillow over her head, jamming it down hard over both ears. Her tongue felt thick, her mouth tasted stale. Her head didn't exactly hurt, but it was definitely fuzzy, consequences of too much wine right before bed. Patra groaned again, this time in remembrance. The latter part of the evening started to replay itself in her mind: the dancing, the hill, the stars, the kisses. Too much wine *and* too much Brennan Carr.

What had she been thinking to have let things get so far out of hand? Oh, never mind. It was a poor rhetorical question. She knew very well what sort of deals she'd made with herself to get what she wanted in the moment last night. Now, she would repent at leisure.

Only there wasn't much leisure about it. The pounding persisted and she let out a loud, frustrated sigh. Good lord, where was that sound coming from? It seemed to be coming straight through the wall. As long as the noise kept up, there would be no leisurely anything. She had to go and see the cause of the commotion. Patra rolled over and gingerly got up, testing the quality of her legs. Unfortunately, they held. The last excuse to remain in bed was gone.

She drew back the white-lace panel covering the bedroom window and let out a startled yelp. Sweet heavens, there was a shirtless man outside her bedroom!

He leaped back, cursing and spitting out nails at her undignified scream. 'Lucifer's balls, woman, do you want me to *swallow* the nails?'

She had a full view of him now. This wasn't just any man standing outside her window. It was Brennan Carr, half-naked, and gorgeously carved; the sculpted muscles of his shoulders and arms, hewn from months of hard work on the boats, the defined planes of his torso narrowing like well-manicured steppes to the waist of his *foustanella*, the journey highlighted by a thin trail of copper hair arrowing to parts lower. It was quite a sight to wake up to. 'What are you doing?' Patra managed to ask once her thoughts reconciled themselves. Gorgeous he might be, but he was also uninvited. Last night wasn't supposed to have led to this. Having him here was the last thing she wanted.

Brennan held up his hammer and offered her a cocky grin. 'I noticed your shutters were loose. I thought I might come by and fix them up.' Part of her wanted to take his arrogance down a notch. It probably hadn't even occurred to him she might throw him off her property. But the other part of her recognised this was an act of neighbourly kindness on his part if she would allow it. Could she?

She looked past him into the scraggly yard where panels of bright blue wood lay on the ground. 'You've done more than nail up some loose shutters.' He'd taken them down and painted them. They looked pretty and bright. Noticeable.

Brennan shrugged as if it were nothing. 'Konstantine had some paint he wasn't using. I thought they could use a little freshening. There was no sense in nailing them back up just to take them down and paint them later. Better to do them now.' He nodded to a wagon parked on the edge of her yard, and the donkey grazing nearby with her goats. 'I brought whitewash, too. I thought I might start on the house once you were up.' He flashed her a smile.

She ought to refuse. She ought to say thank you for the shutters and send him on his way for multiple reasons. The more immediate one being, men who did favours never did them for free. The Englishman would want something in return. After last night, she thought she had a pretty good idea of what that was. If so, he'd be disappointed. She couldn't possibly reciprocate no matter how many shutters he painted. 'Mr Carr, I thank you for your efforts. They are much appreciated. However, I don't want to take you away from your obligations.' Whatever those might be. She had no idea how he spent his days beyond fishing with Konstantine and working Konstantine's booth in the market.

He made an exaggerated show of looking around over his shoulder as if searching for someone. He braced his hand on the house wall and leaned in close to the window. His eyes sparked with mischief. '*Mr Carr?* Really, Patra, who is *that*? You had me thinking my father was here. Last night, you were perfectly content to call me Brennan.'

Patra felt herself smile in spite of the reserve she wanted to maintain. He was positively infectious, irresistible. She tried again, this time more bluntly. 'I don't know exactly what you want, but I have no intentions of sleeping with you in exchange for your services. Some widows might be free with their favours, but I am not one of them.'

He leaned close again, the nearness of him sending a tremor of excitement through her as his words brushed her ear. 'I'll let you in on a little secret, Patra. I don't have to trade services to have a woman in bed. As for what

I want? I'd like a little breakfast if it's not too much trouble.' He glanced out towards the road and shielded his eyes against the sun. 'There's been some traffic on the road this morning.' He gave her one of his considering glances. 'You might want to get dressed. No sense advertising wares that aren't for sale.' He smartly stepped out of reach before she could smack him and went back to work, calling over his shoulder, 'Nothing fancy for breakfast, mind. I like my eggs scrambled.'

He was worried about *her* modesty when *he* was the one strutting about her yard half-naked? Oh, she'd scramble those eggs, all right, right after she added incorrigible to the list of Brennan Carr's descriptors. It was a good thing he was irresistible because that was the only thing saving him from a hand across his face. That and the truth: it had been exciting to find him outside her window.

Patra crossed her arms over her chest in a belated bid for modesty. In the commotion of finding a man outside her window and the visual feeding frenzy of feasting on that man's rather extraordinary physique, she'd forgotten her own; forgotten that she slept in a cotton night-rail that had been quite fine when she'd sewn it seventeen years ago for her trousseau. It had only got thinner over time. It hardly mattered, there was no one to see, but today there *had* been. She was suddenly conscious of the frayed hemming around the neck, the worn fabric. She was conscious, too, of what that thin material might have accidentally re-vealed, of how she must look with her tatty night-rail and sleep-tousled hair, hardly a para-gon of beauty, much like her house. It had been a long time since it had been important to care about either. It had, in fact, been important to give the outward appearance of *not* caring.

Patra retreated into her bedroom, careful to take her clothes behind the screen to dress. She pulled on a loose blouse and a dark skirt and tied on an apron over them. It wasn't that she didn't pay attention to her appearance. She did. Just like the inside of her home was neat and well kept, her appearance was tidy and clean, too. She had not let herself go after Dimitri's death, but she'd had different priorities. She wanted no one's attentions and there were consequences for that. When there was no one to please, no one to appreciate efforts, those efforts simply stopped being made. She missed making those efforts. She'd liked being a wife. But it was one of many things she'd given up to make sure everyone around her was safe, a small price to pay for saving lives.

Patra picked her hairbrush up from the small table that served as her vanity and ran it through her hair. She reached for her hairpins and stopped. Usually, she pinned it up in a tight bun. It was severe but practical for working around the house. Maybe, just for today since she wasn't going anywhere... Patra reached for a ribbon instead. It was dark blue and would hardly be noticeable in her brown hair. Should anyone happen by, no one could criticise her for being too girlish, for standing out and drawing attention.

In the kitchen, she took stock of her supplies. She'd clearly overslept and her morning chores had gone undone. The goats hadn't been milked yet or the chickens seen to, but she had a few eggs left over from yesterday, some bread and half a pitcher of goat's milk.

It would be enough and the animals could wait a short while more.

Patra set about making breakfast, cracking eggs and putting a few pieces of bread on the grill over the fire for toasting, her chagrin over Brennan's comments disappearing as she cooked. She liked to cook, it relaxed her, it centred her. To be honest, she had entertained thoughts of making Brennan's eggs runny and burning the toast just to make a point about his 'wants', but food was hard to come by and while she enjoyed preparing food, it was time consuming—too time consuming not to do it right the first time. Besides, she had her pride. She could hardly have Brennan believing Katerina Stefanos was a better cook.

Not, of course, that it mattered what Brennan thought, she reminded herself as she laid the breakfast tray. She was *not* competing for him. Just because she decided to use a cloth napkin and had picked a blue ceramic plate to serve the eggs on because it brought out their rich yellow colouring, it didn't mean anything. A Greek woman *always* took pride in her hospitality. It had *nothing* to do with a half-naked

Englishman working in her yard. Perhaps it was simply time she started taking pride in the little things again. There was no harm in it. It had been four years, after all. Perhaps it had been enough time.

Those were perilous thoughts and it wasn't the first time she'd entertained them since the moment Brennan had drawn her out on the dance floor. Each grin, each wink, each audacious touch of his, had her thinking she could risk a little more each time, that perhaps she was being overcautious without reason. It was hard to remember the darkness and the danger Castor Apollonius posed when Brennan smiled. Maybe just this once…

Brennan approached the little citrus grove on the edge of the property with its rough-hewn table and chairs, cautiously eyeing the tray Patra set down. Breakfast smelled good, damn good to a man who'd had little sleep and had worked most of the morning through on an empty stomach. He breathed in the morning aroma of toast and eggs. He loved breakfast. It was his favourite meal of the day, his favourite time of day. But he half-expected it to be a trick. He'd made her angry or embarrassed with his comments about her attire, or perhaps she'd been angry before that when she'd assumed he would want something in exchange for his efforts. She'd clearly seen his offer as a bid for what could be delicately termed 'compensated companionship'.

She wasn't entirely wrong. He did want something from her, but not that, at least not in that way. If sex followed, so be it. He wouldn't say no, but the deal he wanted to offer her didn't *require* it. It would be a long time coming before he had to negotiate for sex. Brennan pulled his shirt over his head before settling at the little table, aware that she watched him. He winked and sat down. 'Disappointed? Do you prefer I keep it off?'

Patra laughed, which was what he'd hoped. 'Hardly.'

He grinned over a forkful of eggs. 'Well, don't worry, it's only temporary. I'll take it off again later.'

'Are you always like this?' Patra spread butter on her own toast, a small smile tempting her mouth. She was enjoying this even if she wouldn't admit it.

'Mostly, but I like getting a rise out of you,' Brennan answered boldly. 'It makes you come alive, it makes your eyes light up.' He watched her take in the words. They might be too personal for the brevity of their association, but they were no less true. He'd felt it last night when they'd danced, when they'd kissed, when they'd briefly quarrelled. He wondered when was the last time anyone had prompted such a response from her. 'How long have you been out here alone?' It was a delicate way of asking how long she'd been widowed without being too direct.

'Twelve years this summer.'

Brennan did the maths. She'd been young, twenty-three at most when her husband had passed. They would have had no more than five years together if she'd married at eighteen or seventeen. It wasn't likely she'd married any younger. That meant twelve years of trying to care for this place on her own. No wonder it looked a bit rough. There were a hundred questions he wanted to ask. What kind of man had her husband been? Young like herself? Older? Had he died of illness or natural causes? Disease? How devoted was she to his memory? Did she mean to spend the rest of her life devoted to it? But he knew before asking that those questions were entirely too personal. Instead, he said, 'There's a shed on the corner of the property. It looks like it was once used as a barn of sorts.' Perhaps it would be easier for her to talk about the land.

'Yes, the roof finally caved in last year and I haven't repaired it. The goats have been living outside.'

'I'll do it,' Brennan put in quickly. 'It will only take a couple of days and that way the goats can get out of the olive grove. They'll chew it to sticks if they don't and that won't do your harvest any good come October.' He'd noticed that situation when he'd arrived this morning.

'The grove probably isn't worth saving,' Patra warned him. 'I haven't been able to harvest it in three years beyond what I need for my personal use.'

Brennan leaned forward on his elbows.

'Isn't there anyone in the town to help you?' He was hard pressed to imagine the people of Kardamyli not joining forces to assist someone in need.

Patra stood up and began gathering the plates, apparently done with the conversation and done tolerating his personal questions. He realised his mistake too late. She didn't *want* help and, in her stubbornness, she'd driven off their offers. Now, she was too stubborn to ask for that help back when she needed it.

Brennan rose, too, helping with the dishes. 'Thank you for breakfast, it was most enlightening.'

When she'd gone back inside, Brennan stripped off his shirt, picked up his hammer and went back to work. She would not succeed in driving him off. He needed her compliance too much. But more than that, he had her measure and he knew when someone needed help.

She might chide him for his shirtless attire, but he noticed she couldn't keep her eyes off him. She was spending a lot of time outdoors. She came out to gather eggs. She came out to milk the goats. She came out to check on his progress and to make a few idle suggestions.

In the early afternoon, she came back out with a tray bearing lunch and a slim bottle with a spout on it. They ate pita, filling the bread with goat's cheese and meat.

At the end of the meal, she held up the glass bottle. 'If you insist on not wearing a shirt, you're going to need this.'

'Olive oil?' Brennan looked sceptical, not following her line of reasoning.

'Not just olive oil. You haven't been here yet through a Greek summer or even a spring. You'll have noticed our sun is hot, probably hotter than your English sun. Turn around. Let's get this on your back or you're going to burn.'

Brennan grinned as he gave her his back. He couldn't resist teasing her. 'You can rub my back any time you want, Patra. You don't even need oil.'

Her tone was brisk on purpose and perhaps more severe than required to take away the implication that this was anything more than a necessary task to perform. 'You'll burn without it. Your legs tanned, but you haven't been without a shirt in this sun. I imagine redheads don't tan easily.'

Brennan laughed. 'As a species, that's generally true.' He swiped a finger through the oil on his shoulder, sniffing it. 'Does it work?' Her hands felt cool and capable against his skin.

'It works.' She kneaded his shoulders and he rolled his neck, encouraging her to do it again. 'It protects against damage at least.' He could feel her step back from him. He didn't want her to stop. She passed him the bottle. 'You can do the rest. Cover your chest and your face.'

'I don't know if I have your expertise,' Brennan drawled, knowing full well she'd scold him. Her hands on his chest would be very nice. Still, he had to try.

'You can do it, I have great faith in your oil-applying abilities.' She gave him a wry smile. 'But don't work too much longer. I don't want you fainting from fatigue or heat.'

'Oh, you *do* care.' Brennan grinned, pouring olive oil into the palm of his hand and smearing it on his chest in broad strokes. He watched the pulse at the base of her neck leap. She was definitely *not* indifferent.

'Only because you're too big, I don't think I could drag you inside.' Patra shook her head. 'I'll be in the shade with the mending if you need anything.' Oh, he would. Brennan grinned. He'd make sure of it.

Brennan finished whitewashing the front of the house and began the process of cleaning brushes and putting away the tools, all borrowed from Kon. He wrapped them in an old cloth and stored them in the wagon. He stepped back from the wagon and surveyed his work. The house looked better already. The whitewash made the house gleam under the sun and the blue shutters on the two windows added a crisp finish. He'd get the rest of the house done tomorrow. Right now, there was something else he wanted to do, another project to work on.

He spied Patra under the tree, the mending in her lap. She'd left her hair down today. He'd noticed at breakfast, but he didn't dare comment on it, after the bit with the nightgown. It made her look younger, freer. She wasn't old, she shouldn't dress as if she was. Certainly any mourning obligations to her husband had been satisfied years ago.

Her long chestnut hair hung in a thick skein over one shoulder as she sewed, humming a Greek tune. The domesticity of the scene caught him unawares like a sucker punch to the gut: Patra sewing, the freshly washed house behind her, the olive groves beyond that. They were a tangled mess right now, but they wouldn't be when he'd finished. Come October, they would be healthy again.

He had to stop himself. Would he even be here in October? That was six months away. If he wanted the fantasy he painted in his mind, all he had to do was reach out and claim it with Katerina. It was there for the taking, but he didn't want it with Katerina. That particular fantasy was lacking something.

Did he even want a wife? Last night he had been doing everything he could to avoid such a fate. He wasn't the marrying kind. Marriage was for ever and he could barely manage to do anything for a month. At Oxford, he'd jumped from subject to subject. He'd been fascinated by Aramaic for five weeks and then he'd been fascinated by a merchant's pretty daughter and that had been the end of Aramaic studies. If he'd managed to stay with a subject long enough, he would have been an expert at something instead of a jack of all trades, master of the only one that mattered—sex. Brennan knew how he operated. He had no staying power. Kardamyli was something of an anomaly in that regard. He'd never stayed anywhere this long. He was just infatuated with the moment, with the challenge Patra presented.

Patra looked up, biting off a length of thread. 'Do you need something?'

Brennan grinned, covering up the moment of inner turmoil with nonchalance. 'Yes, I do. I need an answer to my proposition last night.' She gave him a quizzical look, unsure what to say. He stretched out in the grass beside her. 'You know, the one I made right before I kissed you.'

Chapter Six

Of course he would mention *that*. Patra felt her cheeks flush and she struggled to thread her needle. He really didn't play fair. Last night was supposed to exist in a vacuum, it wasn't official, it wasn't supposed to count for anything beyond a momentary escape. How was it that a singular evening had now become the basis for a proposition? A proposition she didn't quite remember. In her defence, she'd been more focused on his mouth at the time than she'd been on the words coming out of it.

Brennan reached over and took the needle from her, threaded it deftly, much to her irritation, and set it aside. 'Perhaps you need a reminder?' His voice was a low seductive ripple of words. 'I believe I was like this.' His body angled close to her as it had been last night, the mere proximity of him sending a heated rush through her. 'My hand was just so.' His palm cupped her jaw, warm and welcoming against her skin. 'My mouth was here—' here being a scant half-inch hovering above hers '—and I said…'

Patra swallowed, his touch doing all sorts of things to her self-control. She remembered now. 'Something about joining forces.' At the time, she hadn't given it much credence, just words murmured in flirtation at a hot moment.

'Well? What do you think? We both have unwanted suitors. By pretending to be together, we can convince them their attentions are futile.' It was hard to resist when his voice was a husky murmur against her throat, his mouth teasing her with its nearness, making her memory crave his kiss. 'It would be worthwhile, Patra.'

Patra summoned the last of her willpower and pulled back. 'Worthwhile for whom? You? What happens when you leave? I will be the poor jilted widow.' That was only the obvious concern. Brennan only thought it would be worthwhile for him. He saw this as a long-term escape from Katerina's clutches.

'For you, too,' Brennan argued, dropping his hand from her cheek. 'You can satisfy the town's desire for you to socially engage while not having to entertain one of those grey-beards under false pretences.'

On the surface, it did look like an expedient solution to the rather pesky problem of her insistent suitors. Still, she wasn't naïve. She doubted his motives were entirely altruistic. 'Somehow I doubt it's that simple,' Patra challenged. 'Do you think to use it as a ploy to land yourself in my bed? Steal a few more kisses?'

'Nothing will happen that you do not wish. What we do inside the privacy of the ruse is up to us alone,' Brennan said solemnly. She believed him as far as that went. He was a rogue, but he had honour. He would never force himself on her. But that was the problem. She highly doubted there'd be any force involved. What if she did wish for something more? Or *thought* she did?

Last night was proof enough that he could

coax a response from her, that she was not immune to the pull of attraction between them. The power of attraction *would* rear its head as it had last night. They could not spend time in one another's presence and remain entirely unaffected. Did she dare explore that pull when it surfaced again? Above all, could she keep Brennan safe from her secrets? Anything more than a temporary association with her could be, well, deadly, if the wrong people heard of it.

And yet, maybe it would be safe enough. How long would Brennan truly stay? Who would tell? The argument from last night rose, joined by the recent mantra that had taken up residence in her mind: *maybe four years was long enough, maybe Castor had let her go.* Brennan was an Englishman, he was leaving. He had no future here, nothing that could be held against him. Castor Apollonius couldn't touch him. Patra shut her eyes and made a quick, silent promise. For a short time at least, she could have what the Englishman offered; a convenient ruse and perhaps a little more should she decide. But only under one condition: she would release him at the first sign of trouble.

Patra swallowed and met his blue eyes. There was a calm reassurance there, encouraging her, persuading her she was going to make the right decision. Did any woman ever say no to him? 'All right, I accept your proposition.'

Brennan leaned in with a wide smile, his hand taking her cheek in a soft caress. 'You won't be sorry.' But he didn't back away.

'What are you doing?' In less than a second it became a rhetorical question. Her body knew what he was doing. Her lips had already parted, her eyes were already half-closed.

'An old English tradition,' he murmured, picking up with his seduction where he'd left off a few moments ago. 'Sealing our deal with a kiss.'

Patra let herself sink into it because she wanted to, because his kisses were intoxicating, and because it was better than the alternative of giving into the small voice of dissent that lingered somewhere in the back of her mind, crying out that she was going to regret this, only to be answered with the response familiar to hedonists everywhere, *but not today.* For now, that was good enough. Today, everything was all sunshine and light.

Modon, on the Peloponnesian Peninsula

Candlelight threw shadows on the stone walls of the dark room, lending a covert air to the meeting as the Grand Master of the Filiki Eteria uttered the words that fired Castor Apollonius's blood. 'There has been a development. I need you to do something for me.' This was what Castor lived for: deadly opportunity. This wasn't the first conversation he'd had with the Grand Master that started this way or took place in such a locale. Secrecy and privacy, were the watchwords of the Filiki Eteria, especially in these times where their power was contested by the new government in Athens. It was a situation Castor was eager to do something about.

Castor inclined his head respectfully towards the man who had spoken. 'I am at your disposal, as always.' He kept his voice calm, but his heart was beginning to race, his adrenaline beginning to flow. At last, the Filiki Eteria, the organisation that had been the success behind the independence movement, was ready to move again. It was about time. The years since the war had not seen the organisation grow in power as anticipated when King Otto took the throne of Greece. Instead, the Filiki Eteria had diminished and King Otto was a mere boy. It was time for the second phase of independence; doing away with the monarchy, or at least with Otto, and setting in his place a man who wasn't controlled by the powers of Europe.

'We need to gather a group of men. It is time to go to Athens.' The Grand Master turned to face him, speaking the words Castor had yearned to hear for years. 'We will need loyal men from the Peloponnese. It is why I have been asked to handle this and why I am asking you to be my emissary.'

Castor acknowledged the compliment with a nod. The men of the Peloponnese had seen the brunt of the fighting during the war. They deserved the honour to serve prominently in this second phase, they'd *earned* the right to be part of the group going to Athens.

'I want you to start in Kardamyli, Brother Castor.' The words took Castor by surprise, but he was careful not to show it. The Grand Master liked cool-headed men, not those guided by passions.

'Why Kardamyli?' It was a bold question to ask the head of the Filiki Eteria in this region. One did not challenge him even when that person ranked as high in the organisation as Castor. He had not been to Kardamyli for four years, although he had men watching the village on occasion. *She* was there, the woman he couldn't forget.

The Grand Master drummed his fingers on the desktop, his eyes on him, studying. 'There are reports of an Englishman lingering there. I thought there might be some help in that for us now that we've decided to make a move against Otto.'

This was not news. Castor's sources had informed him of the Englishman's presence a few months ago when it became evident the man was going to stay around. But it had been of no consequence at the time. There was something more the Grand Master was not telling him. He was going to have to probe for it. 'What is the Englishman to us, sir?'

The Grand Master gave a wry smile. 'He may have information about Britain's willingness to help us.'

Castor lifted his brows. 'You think he's a spy?'

'If he is not, he can be an example. Perhaps he can be used to coax Britain to our aid. I doubt Britain will look favourably on one of their own being killed abroad.'

'Ah, you mean to make a martyr of him?' Castor could see how that would be useful. Britain might think twice about supporting a monarchy that couldn't keep their people safe.

'I want you to take the lead on that.' The Grand Master paused, his words coming slowly. 'There is something else. Our dear, departed Brother Dimitri's widow is still there. She might be of use to us as a translator if she could be persuaded to join us once more. You've always taken a special interest in her. Perhaps you could persuade her, perhaps renew your acquaintance with her.' The Grand Master's tone was mild, as if he didn't guess at the depth of emotions Castor associated with Patra Tspiras.

Castor felt his blood heat at the mention of her. Once, he'd waited for her to finish her grieving, to come to her senses and acknowledge the passion between them, and she had rejected him outright. He absently fingered the hilt of the blade at his belt. He had sworn years ago that if he couldn't have her, no one would.

He bowed to the Grand Master, betraying none of the inward excitement stirring over this mission. 'I will go to Kardamyli. I will leave as soon as arrangements are made.' This time she would not refuse him. He was done playing the gentleman. What he couldn't take by persuasion, he would take by force.

Chapter Seven

To refuse was futile, Patra thought with a laugh, her feet sinking into the sun-warmed sand on the quiet beach. It had been the motto of the week. She'd had a week now to get used to the ruse, to him. But there was so much she hadn't bargained on, such as his constant presence. He made a point of seeing her for part of every day, even if it was simply stepping away from the fish stall just long enough to take a stroll through the market. Of course, she knew it was all for show. No one would believe Brennan had an interest in her or she in him if they weren't seen together. Market strolls were a perfect way to suggest a relationship was budding, the natural product of having shared a dance which had led to doing a few repairs around her home.

Brennan had masterminded a very believable progression of their relationship for all to see and he was careful not to push the boundaries of propriety in public. But they were not always in public. That was when she had to remind herself it was all a ruse, an act, most particularly on days like today when there was no one to perform for and it was far too easy to forget.

Water lapped at Patra's toes, covering them with warm waves. Brennan had wanted to go swimming and so they had. It was outrageous and potentially scandalous: swimming. *With* Brennan Carr. She could add that to the growing list of things she shouldn't have done but had.

Brennan had been quite persuasive. It was too hot to work this afternoon, the beach was a hidden cove, no one would see, he'd said, flashing her an irresistible smile and holding out a hand to help her up on the narrow seat of his borrowed work wagon. So here she was, toes digging into the sand, waves pushing against her feet and her pulse racing because one never knew what Brennan would do next, or what he'd invite *her* to do next.

This week, she'd discovered it wasn't so much what Brennan did that was scandalous as much as what he got others to do. She was leading herself down a dangerous path; first dancing, then star-gazing, sharing meals and now this. She recognised he hadn't broken his word that nothing would happen she didn't desire. She couldn't help herself and it just seemed to get easier and easier as the choices grew. The problem wasn't Brennan, it was her, all her. *She* was making choices that created intimacy. And now, apparently, nudity.

At the water's edge, Brennan was already stripping out of his shirt and tossing it aside with unabashed glee at the prospect of the sea. His joy reminded her of a child let out of school for an unexpected holiday. It made her smile and it made her jealous. When was the last time she'd felt that carefree? Watching him shed his shirt stirred her own hunger. She wanted to claim that same freedom for herself, too.

He didn't stop there. He let the *foustanella* drop to the sand just beyond the water, offering her an unobstructed view of firm, muscled buttocks. They were marble hard, a sculptor's delight—and a woman's. Who wouldn't want to run a hand over such a masterpiece? She could see the horizontal line of color that delineated those white buttocks from the tan of his uncovered back.

Brennan glanced over his shoulder, unbothered by her gaze. 'Are you coming or are you just going to stand there and look?' Something he clearly wouldn't mind, she realised. He was comfortable with himself, confident in his body with clothes or without. It was an earthy trait, not something she'd have expected from a gentleman, certainly not the gentlemen officers she'd met during the war.

'Well?' Brennan challenged with a grin. 'Come on!' The envy she'd felt became yearning. She wanted nothing more than to be like him, to be confident in her body the way she had been once. To revel in what her body offered instead of fear it. Twelve years was a long time to hide. If this week had proven refusal was futile, it had perhaps also proven that she was safe now. Castor had moved on. She should move on, too.

The decision made her exultant. Here on this beach, with this man, she would shed the last of the chains of the past. She favoured Brennan with a smile that answered his challenge and reached for her shoes, then her stockings. Her skirt fell and she pulled her loose cotton blouse over her head, until she stood on the beach wearing only her chemise.

'That's so much better.' Brennan's grin was infectious as he held out his hand. 'I'll race you in!' She slipped her hand in his, and they began to run, splashing and laughing in the warm waves. In an instant, swimming actually became about swimming. Any self-consciousness over nakedness or wet, revealing chemises evaporated in the wake of the magic conjured up by these waves. This was living, this was *fun*. She felt reborn in the waters, a part of her experiencing this freedom for the first time.

Brennan executed a shallow dive and disappeared under the surface. Only then did she realise she hadn't looked at him, except for his buttocks. The realisation spoke volumes about the nature of this expedition. Perhaps it was possible that a man and woman could have fun together without it having to mean something sensual?

Brennan surfaced several yards away and broke into a crawl stroke that showcased the muscles of his arms, the sleek athleticism of his body as it cut through the water. She abruptly rescinded her position. No. It was not possible. He was showing off for her now, but it made her grin. Maybe Brennan couldn't help it. Everything was a big flirt to him, even her, even inside the parameters of this make-believe arrangement. Maybe that was all right. Why not flirt, why not enjoy one another's company as long as it was safe? And it was.

Patra dived beneath the water and swam out after him. She had some showing off to do, too.

They swam together, daring each other to silly races. They dived beneath the surface to swim with the colourful little fish. The waves were calm, the water warm and they were in no hurry for it to end. When they were exhausted, they flipped on to their backs and let their bodies bob on the waves. The sun was starting its slow descent by the time they decided to swim back to the beach. Their towels and a blanket waited, warm from the afternoon. Brennan wrapped his around his waist and stretched out on the blanket. 'This is all I need: a beach, some sand, water, a blanket or two.' He gave her a melting smile. 'And a lovely woman to share it with.'

Patra wrapped her towel about her and sat beside him, but she could feel her own awareness of their rather clothesless state start to return. Perhaps it had been his words. She shoved the self-conscious feeling aside, trying to hold on to the magic as long as possible. She looked out over the water. To look at him would be too potent. She feared it would wreck what was left of the magic. 'You surprise me. You're not like any gentlemen I know. They have to have their estates, their fortunes. Their lives are too complicated to settle for beaches and sand.'

Brennan chuckled. 'You're a lady of mystery, Patra. What do you know of English gentlemen?' he teased. 'I think you've been holding out on me.'

'There were British officers on the peninsula during the war. We encountered a few,' she offered, turning to give him a brief glance.

'Is that how you learned English?' Brennan propped himself into a half-reclining position, levered up on one arm.

Patra nodded. 'Translators were a rare commodity this far from Athens and I had an aptitude for it.'

A little wall of silence sprung up between them. Brennan's voice was quiet, serious, when he breached that wall with tentative solemnity. 'You were involved in the war then. Is that how you lost your husband?'

The hesitancy of his tone suggested he recognised he was pushing the boundaries of polite conversation. But, Patra thought, why not push that boundary as well when the two of them had pushed so many limits already today? She played with the fringe of the blanket, plaiting it into little braids. Perhaps this was part of her new freedom, acknowledging the past instead of hiding from it. 'Yes. Early 1825. He was with Ibrahim, Mehmet Ali's son, in the fight at the Turkish stronghold of Modon. The Turks on the peninsula had no intention of going easily and we had no intentions of letting them stay.'

Brennan nodded gravely. 'The scorched-earth campaign. I've heard of it, very intense.'

'How did you guess?' She hazarded a sideways look at him, fearing she'd see pity in his eyes.

Brennan shrugged, but his eyes held hers, not letting her gaze leave him. 'You aren't made for an old man, Patra. Your husband had to be young, too.'

'I'm thirty-five, Brennan, five years older than you, hardly a girl in the first blush of youth.' Not like Katerina Stefanos, who was twenty and had parents who guarded her virtue like wardens. Patra had no such virtue left.

Brennan scoffed at the idea. 'If thirty-five is too young to live life like a nun, then twenty-three certainly is. You can't mean to throw your life away on your husband's memory, not when there is so much life left in you, *for* you.' His quiet tone gentled the words. It wasn't the first time she'd heard that message. The women in the village had been preaching it for two years now. Apparently, ten years was the statute of limitations on grieving. Too bad that didn't seem to apply to forgetting, as well. She didn't want to forget Dimitri, but she did want to forget what had happened to him and why. She didn't want to remember that it had been her fault he'd died. But it wasn't a choice. Remembering was her penance. All the freedom in the world couldn't change that.

'I suppose you think I should experience that life with you? That I should throw my reputation away on a young man like yourself who will be here and gone whenever the mood strikes him?' She felt her anger start to rise, encroaching on her euphoria. What did Brennan know of loss and sacrifice in his gilded life? 'You presume too much on too short of an acquaintance.' Patra tried to stand. Perhaps it would be best to return home before the day was ruined.

Brennan's hand closed around her wrist. She felt a *frisson* of thrill shoot up her arm like it always did when he touched her. It didn't matter where they were. It could be the simplest of touches, a hand at her elbow in the market, and it would still ignite her as if it were the most intimate of caresses. 'Patra, don't do this.'

'Don't do what? I'm merely standing up.' She was trying to resist, truly she was.

'Stop it, please.' Brennan tugged her down gently and she took up her place on the blanket. 'You're walking away physically and verbally. You do this when the conversation becomes difficult.' She wanted to argue. She'd never walked away from anything, but Brennan continued, not giving her a chance to respond. 'You did it that first night on the hill, you did it when I showed up to paint your shutters and you're doing it now. You don't want to talk about the past and you don't want to explore your own needs, so you create a quarrel.'

Every sense she possessed flared with danger: *fight, fight, fight, he is too close.* Had anyone in the past twelve years seen her as clearly as he saw her right now? It was positively frightening and yet beautifully bittersweet that of all the people in the world who had the capacity to really see her, it was an Englishman who was merely passing through her life, who could mean nothing to her. But that was for later. Right now, Brennan's blue eyes had become the sum of her world as they held her gaze, urging her to listen.

'Don't be afraid of what I make you feel. To be truly free, Patra, you have to own your past, not just the facts, but the emotions, too. Otherwise, you can't give yourself the future you deserve.' She was acutely aware this was real. This moment, these words, were not part of a ruse. They were for her, outside any fiction the two of them were creating. The realisation nearly choked her.

'How do you know such a thing?' Patra whispered. Their heads were close together, their voices hushed with the divine intimacy of the moment. She could hear the quiet susurration of the waves just beyond them.

'Because I've been there,' Brennan murmured, his confession brushing her lips, his mouth close to hers.

In that moment, she wanted to know. She

whispered her own question against his lips. 'How? Tell me.' What had he struggled against? What ghosts could possibly haunt this glorious man-boy's past?

There were no answers, only the sliding of his mouth over hers in a communion of sinners, two flawed persons searching for salvation. He pressed her back on the blanket, his body covering hers. This, she recognised, was his strategy; to offer physical intimacy in lieu of conversation. It was not a poor substitute.

Blue eyes looked down at her, wet auburn hair framed his sun-kissed face, a slow, intensely private smile taking his mouth, muscled arms bracketing her head. Her breath came fast. There was going to be trouble, *good* trouble. She wanted to reason she hadn't bargained on this, but deep down she knew she had.

'Let me give you what you need.' He was asking permission not only for himself. He didn't need it. He was probably very aware he could coax compliance from her. He was asking on her behalf. She needed to give herself permission, out loud, with witnesses.

She breathed a single word. 'Yes.'

Brennan's mouth took hers again, not in invitation as his first had been, but in affirmation of her permission. She welcomed the press of his lips, the exploration of his tongue, the weight of his body, warm and male atop her. His hips moved against hers in the smallest of motions, but it was enough to ignite certain fires. She moaned a sigh as his hand slid beneath her wet chemise to claim a breast in a slow caress. It was his turn to groan, his mouth moving to feast at her neck, to the valley between her breasts. His hands were at her hips, pushing up the clingy chemise, pushing aside the clumsily wrapped towel.

His mouth kissed her navel, foreshadowing his intentions, giving her the choice and she gave it, her body opening to him in its most private arenas. How unnerving, how exquisite, that he'd known precisely what she needed.

He slipped his hand between her thighs, resting it in the curls of her mound. She could feel her body quiver and then steady itself as he murmured soft words of encouragement. It had been so long since she'd felt like this, *wanted* to feel like this. His fingers moved, finding her slick pearl. He drew his thumb over it, a slow, sure caress that tantalised, bringing her closer to some nebulous edge with every pass. Her moans came in short gasps now, her body desperate for the promise that awaited it.

'Let go, Patra. Let it come, invite it to take you,' Brennan's voice coaxed, compelling and smooth, sure. She could trust that voice. He would not fail her, not in this. 'This is just another cliff, Patra. *Jump.* Jump for me.'

And she did. But she did not merely jump, she *flew* with the sun setting in a blue-violet sky above her, the last of the sand's afternoon warmth at her back, her lover's hand on her, calling forth release. Her body remembered *this* and it called forth memories of its own, it unlocked self-imposed chains. Somewhere in the last twelve years she'd forgotten her true self, the passionate, vibrant woman who embraced life. That woman was still there, locked away deep inside for reasons Patra couldn't remember just now with Brennan's hand at her core, with her passion rising, with release seizing her in its fevered pitch. What she did know was that in these moments, she was free. The little voice in her mind that cried caution was silent at last.

Chapter Eight

In those shattering moments, Brennan knew a primal satisfaction. Patra was beautiful in her pleasure, her throat exposed, her head thrown back. Who would have guessed such depths of passion lay beneath the stoic woman he'd seen in the market? Patra wore vulnerability well and it moved something ancient and possessive at the core of him. To make oneself vulnerable was to trust, and in these seconds, Patra trusted him. It was quite remarkable given that she'd been fighting every step of the way. But he'd recognised it wasn't him she was fighting, it was herself.

He smoothed back her hair and placed a soft kiss at her temple. 'Now you know it's possible. You can stop fighting.'

'I'm not fighting anyone,' she murmured, her voice drowsy, her eyes dreamy when they met his.

'You're fighting yourself.' Brennan settled beside her, body stretched out, head propped in a hand. 'Trust me, I've seen this fight enough to know what it looks like.' His free hand traced idle circles on the flat of her stomach. 'My friend Haviland fought it when he resisted the marriage his family arranged and traded it for the marriage he wanted with the woman he loved. My friend Archer fought it when his mother died. How could he be true to her and still be true to his family? These are important questions for men of honour. The answers will drive their lives. It's an important fight to win because it will determine whether or not they will have the only thing in life that matters.'

'What's that?' She smiled at him and he felt a very different answer in his gut. *You. You could be the sole focus of a man's life and he would consider it a success.* But that was just fanciful wishing brought on by the sea and the sun and perhaps the echoes of domesticity from the day.

'Happiness,' Brennan answered. 'Happiness is the only thing that matters.'

'Not love?' She wanted to debate, he could see her eyes starting to spark with some mischief, her drowsiness leaving her.

'Love is a form of happiness.' He looked out over the water where the sun hung, a big fiery orb on the horizon before it plunged into the water. 'Count with me, Patra. Let's put the sun to bed.'

She sat up and he wrapped an arm about her, drawing her close against his side, her head on his shoulder, elusive happiness filling him. He'd found it for a moment. He didn't expect it to last much longer, but he'd learned to take what he could get. Her soft voice joined his. 'Five, four, three, two…one. Goodnight, sun.'

Patra tossed her head, drawing her hair to one side over a shoulder. She gave him a contemplative stare, thoughts moving behind her dark eyes. 'Do you think someone can find love, a strong abiding love, more than once in a lifetime?' If Katerina Stefanos had asked him that question, he would have run screaming.

But from Patra it was non-threatening. She wasn't angling for him. They had their agreement and aside from what happened here on the beach, she wasn't emotionally ready. Neither of them wanted to marry at the moment. She was not asking because of any feelings between the two of them. She was asking for herself. 'I wonder sometimes if my husband was my one and only grand passion, would I be wrong to try and look for it with another? If he was my one chance, then perhaps it is futile to even search because it won't be out there.'

'I don't know,' Brennan said slowly, honestly. Stars were starting to come out in the lavender sky. 'I don't even know if we get the assurance of finding such a thing even once.'

'Ah, I see.' There was a tinge of sorrow in the undertone of her voice. 'You've never been in love.'

'Not yet.' A pale star shot across the sky and Brennan closed his eyes. 'But I keep hoping.'

Was he looking for love? The thought haunted him long after he'd taken Patra home and returned to his room in Konstantine's guest quarters. Was love the reason he was still travelling south long after his friends had stopped? Was he literally leaving no rock unturned in his search? He hadn't thought of it in that way before. He'd understood he had been looking for fun, for adventure. Had those things merely been a mask for something superficial, ways to fill a deeper need?

Brennan stretched and got off his bed. He was too awake to sleep even after all the exercise and the early morning. His mind was alive and busy, a sure sign he wouldn't sleep any time soon. He was used to it. He ate like the proverbial horse and he slept like one, too. Archer had taught him that years ago in school. Horses could survive on two hours of sleep a night. Brennan laughed to himself as he climbed the stairs to Kon's rooftop patio. Two hours sounded just about right and why not? He was a firm believer he'd get all the sleep he needed when he was dead. Until then, there was too much to do.

'Did I miss the joke?' Konstantine turned from the railing.

'No, I was just thinking about horses.' Brennan joined him, leaning his elbows on the railing and staring out to the harbour. He could see Kon's boat from here. Too bad London homes didn't have this feature. He loved the rooftop patio; cool and private, a place where a man could gather his thoughts at the end of the day.

'I'm surprised you aren't thinking about women instead.' Konstantine gave him a friendly elbow to the ribs, but his tone was serious. 'It seems you must truly be irresistible if you have even the remote Patra Tspiras at your feet. Not even the great war hero, Castor Apollonius, managed to capture her affections. Not that the village ever considered that a tremendous loss.' Konstantine leaned on his elbows, staring out to the harbour. 'The two of them broke over politics, it appears. He wanted to support a, um, certain organisation, shall we say, in the new government and she didn't. He persisted with that political stance and she would have nothing to do with him. She retreated from our little society after that. Everyone was surprised.'

'Why?'

'He's wealthy, powerful, handsome and he'd been especially close to her husband,' Konstantine explained. 'He was with her husband when he died. It seemed to many of us grief would have brought them together.' A little flame of irrational jealousy sparked out of nowhere in Brennan's gut. Another man had wanted Patra and had actively pursued her.

Konstantine paused and Brennan sensed there was more his friend wanted to say. It had been a week since the party, a week since Katerina had made her bold play for him. Brennan thought he knew what it was his friend wanted to ask. 'I don't intend to marry Katerina Stefanos,' Brennan said quietly in the dark. 'The offer is very generous and I am cognisant of the honour the family's attentions do me, especially as an outsider. But I can't make her happy.' Couldn't make *himself* happy, not with her. He didn't have much to offer a wife, but he could at least offer happiness. He would hold on to that.

Kon was patient with him, his nod slow and understanding in the dark. 'Are you sure? It is a perfect offer. It would set you up for life.'

Brennan swallowed. 'I know.' With Katerina he would have the simple life he wanted, a life where he worked with his hands and mind to create a product. There would be joy in bringing in the olive harvest every year, in nurturing the groves, watching over them all year, making his own money. 'I do wonder why I can't say yes and be done with it.' Brennan sighed. 'Sometimes I think there is something fundamentally wrong with me.'

Konstantine laughed. 'There is nothing wrong with you that hasn't plagued every man who has not yet met his match. You don't love Katerina and you are unwilling to resign yourself to a life without that one thing.' But his laughter was short-lived.

Konstantine blew out a breath. 'I don't mean to tell you what to do, but you are new here and you may need some guidance. The village does not care that you have chosen not to marry Katerina. There was nothing official, nothing publicly agreed to. But the village does want you to marry someone if you stay.'

Brennan waited patiently. This was not new. He'd sensed it for a few weeks now, this shift in the village's expectations of him. It was what had driven him to the ruse with Patra.

Konstantine shook his head. 'I don't think Patra can be that woman.'

Brennan felt a surge of protectiveness well up. 'Why not?' It came out more defensively than he'd anticipated.

'I don't know.' Konstantine was struggling to find words, wanting to be blunt, but wanting to respect him, too. 'I think she's hiding something. Something keeps her apart from us, something more than the grief of losing her husband.' He clapped a hand on Brennan's shoulder. 'I am glad she is allowing you to help her. The place needs it. We all offered at one time or another, but…' He sighed, letting his words trail off with implication.

Hadn't he, too, sensed Patra's reticence stemmed from something more? Hadn't that been the very reason he'd offered the bargain in the first place? She wasn't in a position to accept more from him than this temporary alliance. It prevented him from having to offer more. And that had been fine right up until today. The beach…well, the beach had been a revelation to say the least. Now, here he was, jealous of a spurned suitor he'd never met.

'I think worry is premature. I've only squired her about the market and done a few repairs.' He opted for nonchalance, hoping he was compelling. Guilt dug its spurs into Brennan's gut. He hated misleading his friend. Kon was only telling him all of this because Kon had fallen for the ruse, the village was falling for it and Kon wanted to warn his friend. 'I'll be careful, Kon. Thanks for the advice.'

He meant it. Konstantine had become a true friend in the last six months, giving him a room in his home, giving him a job on the fishing boat and insisting he take some small wage. He understood the job paid him in other ways, too; it gave his days purpose and structure, it gave his body something to do that it was good at and it paved the way to his acceptance in a socially closed community that viewed strangers with distrust. Brennan owed Kon and his wife, Lydia, far more than could be paid back with something as common as money.

'I just don't want to see you hurt,' Kon replied, pushing off the railing. 'Now, if you'll excuse me, Lydia is waiting.' He winked and headed for the stairs. He paused before going down. 'You can do what you want, Brennan. I just wanted you to know Patra is a woman in need, but she is also alone because she wants to be.'

Brennan nodded and watched his friend go. Maybe he should stop looking for love. That was how it had happened for Haviland, for Archer, for Nolan. Love had found them. They had not found it. He certainly wasn't looking for love with Patra Tspiras. He merely wanted to buy some time, wanted to figure out where he went from here. At least that's what he told himself, because if that wasn't the answer, he wasn't sure what was. Life was good at the moment. That would have to be enough.

Chapter Nine

Life was good at the moment and it was more than enough for Patra as she took a leisurely stroll through the market. Her basket was nearly full, but she wasn't ready to leave. It was mid-morning and the agora was bustling beneath mild blue skies, a light breeze blowing gossip.

Her eyes and ears drifted towards Konstantine's fish stall. She wasn't alone in her attentions. Most of the market's customers were entertained by the display. Konstantine and Brennan were in the stall, shirtless, making an impressive pair as they tossed full-sized fish back and forth to each other, filling orders and keeping up a humorous patter with the crowd as they worked. An occasional 'Omppah!' broke out followed by applause over a difficult catch.

'How many fish today, Kiria Pachis?' Brennan called out to an older woman in the crowd, a wealthy widow Patra knew.

'The biggest one you have! I want to watch those muscles work!' she called back while the crowd cheered.

Konstantine held one up for her inspection. 'How is this?' He hefted a large fish and threw it to Brennan, who made quite a show of catching it and quickly slicing it open. The crowd oohed and ahhed over the speed at which Brennan deboned the fish and wrapped it. He was mesmerising, an artist at work. She'd never watched him do that before.

'Your handsome man is putting on quite a show.' Konstantine's wife, Lydia, came up and slipped a friendly arm through hers with a sly grin. 'The fish throwing is something new they've started,' Lydia whispered. 'Brennan told Kon he thinks it will be good for sales if they make buying fish into a show.' Patra didn't know if it made *that* much difference. People were going to buy fish no matter what.

But if it made the task more enjoyable, who was she to argue?

Brennan deboned another fish, his long filleting knife flashing in quicksilver motions, and she was as entranced as the rest of the crowd. Lydia whispered to her, 'Personally, I think your handsome man could sell salt to the sea.'

Patra felt herself blush. 'He's not my handsome man.' She tried to deny it out of reflex, but Lydia tossed her a knowing smile.

'Are you sure? I can think of worse men to claim.' Lydia tightened her grip on Patra's arm, flashing her easy smile to everyone they passed, making it clear Patra was with her as always. Nothing had changed. Patra was grateful for the support. If Lydia was willing to accept the idea of her with Brennan, others might be more amenable to the idea, too.

'I worried people might be upset about Brennan not declaring for Katerina,' Patra confessed.

Lydia shrugged. 'Nothing official was declared and Brennan behaved honourably with her. I think the town is more interested in him staying instead of who he stays with or for. He's been good for us. Everyone likes him.' She squeezed Patra's arm. 'If it's you, so much the better. You deserve to be happy.' Lydia lowered her voice confidentially. 'Don't worry about Katerina. She'll find a husband. Pretty girls like her always do.'

Patra managed a smile, but guilt haunted her. Lydia was her friend, had been her friend since she'd first come to the village. They'd been new brides together. Konstantine and Dimitri had fished together on occasion. Then Dimitri had died and distance had sprung up between them. Patra had been absorbed into the village's circle of widows, older women, while Lydia had a husband and children, part of a different set of the village's social life. They saw each other only occasionally over the years, at gatherings like market day or church, or Konstantine's birthday party. Their friendship might be different these days, but it sat sorely with Patra that Lydia was unwittingly supporting a ruse.

Brennan spotted her in the crowd, his eyes holding hers, a wide grin spreading across his face, and she felt herself blush. It didn't feel like a ruse when he looked at her like that. 'Kon!' Brennan called out, tossing a fish his friend's direction. 'You know what they say, "Teach a man to fish and he feeds himself for a lifetime". But do you know what they say when you *give* a woman a fish?'

'No, what do they say?' Kon caught the slippery fish by the tail.

'They say she'll invite you to dinner!' Brennan's voice boomed out over the crowd, chuckling at them all. The crowd laughed with him.

'Give me a fish and you can come to dinner all month!' a woman called good-naturedly.

Patra felt Brennan's gaze fall on her, giving her a moment's warning before he flashed the full power of his smile at the woman. 'I'm sorry, dear lady, I'm already spoken for.' It was neatly done. What better way to make their association public knowledge than to humorously announce it? Of course, there was some discretion. He didn't outright name any names, which was best. Anyone who truly needed to know, would know it was her.

There was an outburst of exaggerated sighs

of disappointment and calls of advice, which Brennan accepted good-naturedly. Something stirred in her at the sight of him with Konstantine, with the villagers. He was one of them, they treated him as if he belonged and he acted as if he did. Was that pride she felt? Was it possession? Maybe it was a combination of both that made her throat tight. Or maybe yesterday on the beach had changed more than she thought.

Lydia elbowed her in the ribs. 'Not yours, hmm? I don't think he shares that opinion.' Lydia squeezed her arm in farewell. 'I think he's good for you. Don't be afraid to let yourself be happy, Patra. You've mourned Dimitri long enough,' she said before moving off into the crowd.

Patra smiled to herself. She *was* happy. Being with Brennan made her happy, she realised, although that couldn't last. It wasn't meant to. But the other piece of her happiness could last, the piece that came from deciding to let go of the past, to not let it chain her. She'd given enough years of her life to fear.

Patra stood to the side of the crowd and

watched Brennan work, watched him flirt outrageously with the customers. Lydia was right—he was good for the village. He was so vibrant and alive, how could anyone not be drawn to him? Not want to be in his sphere? She wondered if he knew how magnetic he was, or how much he'd done for the village simply by being here? It was no surprise the village was eager to keep him.

Perhaps if she hadn't been so caught up in her daydreams, and newfound happiness, she might have felt the approach of evil before its long shadow fell over the path, before its voice spoke low and private at her ear, destroying in one damning sentence the happiness she'd so recently claimed. 'The Filiki haven't heard from you in a while, my dear.'

Castor Apollonius. She would know that low, gravelled voice anywhere. All the heat, all the joy, went out of the bright day. She could feel him behind her now: tall, physically imposing, daunting. The rush of thoughts were the only things that kept the overwhelming terror he invoked in her at bay. She would *not* look at him. She would *not* satisfy him with even the smallest of glances. She kept her eyes fixed on Brennan instead, on bright copper hair, on laughing blue eyes and bulging muscles. Her mind reeled, searching for a strategy. 'There has been nothing to report.' She must remain aloof, must not let him see her fear.

'Nothing but an Englishman who refuses to leave. I can't imagine what sort of charms a tiny fishing village on the coast of nowhere holds for such a man,' he replied. 'Surely you know how interesting that bit of news would be to the brotherhood.'

A cold finger of fear travelled down her spine in spite of the warm day. Castor was here for Brennan. All her protective instincts surged. Brennan was watching her, watching them. His patter had become less enthusiastic. His smile had faded. 'The Englishman is nothing,' Patra responded coolly. Perhaps Castor would leave if she could convince him Brennan was not a person of interest. How hard could it be especially when it was the truth? 'Living here is a novelty for him as he takes a break from his Grand Tour. He fishes and he flirts, that is all.'

Castor's hand trailed down her arm in a caress. She fought the urge to flinch. How dare he touch her, how dare he attempt to lay any sort of public claim to her? 'Does he flirt with you?' It was not a businesslike question.

A lie would only make the situation worse. Patra opted for a semblance of the truth. 'He flirts with everyone.' She jerked her head towards the fish stall. 'All you have to do is watch him and you know it's true. Every woman between sixteen and sixty swoons with delight over him.' Brennan chose that moment to outrageously tease old Granny Anastas long enough to slip an extra package of much-needed fish into her basket without her noticing—some of Konstantine's crab legs, if Patra were to guess. No one needed the food more and no one would take charity less.

Behind her, Castor was silent. She could feel him thinking, could hear him breathing. She could imagine his dark eyes narrowing in contemplation as he watched Brennan. 'Perhaps he should flirt with you. You should encourage it,' he said in silky tones. During the war, he'd charmed plenty of women with that voice. He lifted the long skein of her hair, letting it fall through his fingers. 'You're wearing it down again. I like it that way, it's very becoming. You're a beautiful woman, Patra, even when you try to hide it.' He draped her hair over her shoulder, letting it fall against her breast.

She wanted to scream, wanted to kick, to lash out. But to what end? He *knew* how much she loathed him, just as he knew precisely what he was doing to her with these possessive touches. She could not give him the satisfaction of an emotional outburst. 'I am too old for him. The Englishman is young.' She feigned nonchalance. Brennan *did* look young today, with his unruly hair falling in his face, his waves wild as he worked.

'A man in his prime, I'd say. I wouldn't think he'd be too picky. A man has needs,' Castor cajoled, the back of his hand skimming her jaw. She did flinch then, the touch far too intimate.

'Take your hands off me.'

'Or what?' Castor gave a low, cruel chuckle. 'There's no one here who will gainsay me.

Who do you think will rescue you? I'm a good catch for you, Patra. I'm wealthy and handsome. There's nothing I wouldn't give you. I could take you away from this life of hard work and scrabbling for existence if you would give me a chance.' He sighed, nostalgia lacing his voice. 'You used to be my best source, Patra. The Filiki hope you will be again. It's part of the reason why I'm here.'

'And the other part? Why else are you here?' She needed information. Was he passing through? Was he here on a mission? Had the Filiki decided to move against the king in Athens or was this visit personal?

The back of his hand stroked her arm rhythmically. 'There are so many reasons why I'm here. Business, pleasure, you. It's time you and I renewed our acquaintance, I think. Four years is a long space. I have a parlour set aside at the tavern. Come with me and we will talk.'

Patra said nothing, letting the silence communicate her disdain. She would not bargain privacy for information. She would never allow herself to be alone with him again.

He pulled at her arm, trying to force her compliance. 'You admired me once, Patra, don't forget that.' She had and it had been one of her grossest misjudgements. Her temper had reached its limit. Patra yanked at her arm, attempting to free it from his grip. She'd forgotten how strong he was, how big. He merely laughed. But in the next moment, there was a surge of movement, a blur of physical action. Brennan leapt the fish counter, knife in hand, the point coming up against Castor's jaw.

'Take your hands off the lady.' Brennan's voice was a fierce growl, his body tense and ready for battle. She'd not seen him like this. Gone was the carefree, boyish charmer. In his place was a warrior, armed and willing to fight. A primal satisfaction coursed through her at the thought. He wasn't just any warrior. He was *her* warrior. Castor had not been planning on that. There would be hell to pay for it later, but for now she felt redeemed.

Brennan's free hand closed over her arm and drew her away from Castor, shoving her behind him to the edge of the crowd, to the edge of the booth. But Castor wasn't quite subdued. 'Easy, boy.' He held out his hands in a gesture of surrender. 'The lady and I were just talking. We're old friends. There is no need to draw weapons.' He said the last with a touch of sarcasm as if to belittle the boning knife Brennan held to his jaw. The crowd gave a nervous half-hearted laugh, unwilling to desert Brennan and yet unwilling to go against Castor.

Brennan pressed the blade hard enough to draw a bead of blood. 'I'll be the judge of that.' Patra wanted to lunge forward, wanted to tug his hand and tell him to put the knife away, but it would only make it look as if she was pleading on Castor's behalf, something she was unwilling to do.

She was relieved to see Konstantine step forward, a hand on Brennan's shoulder. 'Captain, forgive him, he's not from around here. This is Brennan Carr...' Konstantine began, trying to smooth things over. 'Brennan, this is Captain Castor Apollonius, one of the heroes of the late war.'

Brennan's knife came down, but the muscles in his back did not ease. Still, Patra breathed a little easier. The crisis was over, for now. She took one step back and then another and another until she was on the periphery of the agora. Then, she turned and ran, the fear that she'd held at bay in the market overwhelming her at last.

She let her brain acknowledge the facts of the past quarter-hour. Castor was here! Her worst nightmare had come to life. She'd been wrong about everything. She wasn't free at all and now her very actions put Brennan at risk. It was hard to breathe by the time she got home. Sobs mixed with great gasping gulps of exertion. Her hands shook as she knelt and reached under her bed and pulled out a long wooden box. Her only thought was that she had to load the guns.

Oh, what a fool she'd been! Fate had played the cruellest of tricks on her. She'd allowed herself to be happy, allowed herself to dream just a little and then fate had yanked the rug out from under her. Her hands began to steady as they went through the old routine of priming, her breathing slowed as anger fought back against the fear. She cocked the trigger on one gun and then the other with a sense of finality. The past had come again, but this time, she'd be ready for it.

Chapter Ten

This was a new and most unwelcome development, Castor mused, pacing his makeshift office in the tavern parlour. Patra had a champion. He didn't like that at all. Patra was *his*. She had been for twelve years, ever since Dimitri had died, and now this upstart Englishman threatened to steal her. The Englishman would have to learn what other men foolish enough to court Patra had already learned to their grave misfortune: if he couldn't have Patra Tspiras, no one could.

'I want to know everything about Brennan Carr,' Castor barked to his secretary, a tall thin man with a penchant for cruelty that equalled Castor's own. 'We can do nothing until I know for certain what he is.' If Carr was a British informant, he would have to deal more subtly with him than if he was only what Patra claimed—a man on holiday. Castor couldn't very well kill off the man sent to help the Filiki. Although there had been no word out of Athens that the British were considering action against King Otto, it wasn't beyond the realm of possibility.

'I can't stay,' Castor told his secretary, 'but I will expect a full report when I return.' Castor shoved clothing into a saddle bag. He had other villages to visit, other informants to check with. Was the Peloponnese ready to rise again? Ready for the next stage of independence?

It was his mission to determine that level of readiness. As much as that mission appealed to him, he would rather have stayed in Kardamyli and tracked Brennan Carr himself. 'I'll be back within a week. Arrange a banquet for me when I return. We need to remind the citizens of the glory of the war, not the cost. Make sure the most influential citizens are invited and make sure Patra Tspiras and the Englishman are on the guest list.'

Castor supposed it didn't matter what the Englishman was in the long run. When he returned to Kardamyli, Patra would be leaving with him whether she liked it or not. He would give her the chance to come willingly, of course. But if not, the Filiki had ways of dealing with those who were not loyal to the order. Patra had not reported the Englishman's presence. It wouldn't take much to trump up charges against her. The threat of a Filiki trial would make her eager for any assistance he could provide. Separated from her village and facing execution for treason, she would be alone except for him.

Of course, the charges would never stick. Patra wasn't a member, merely the widow of a member. But it would be enough to get her out of town and that was all that mattered. When she was free of the charges, thanks to his own efforts on her behalf, he'd remind her this was the second time he'd stood between her and disaster. She would learn to be grateful. *Very grateful*. Castor made a subtle adjustment to his tightening trousers, reminding himself that not yet, but soon, his desires would be fulfilled. Patra would yet come to see him as a friend, as a lover, not the enemy.

'It seems you may have made an enemy,' Konstantine said grimly as Brennan looked about the now-quiet marketplace. There wouldn't be any more customers today. Everyone was too unsettled to focus on shopping. Shoppers had slipped out of the marketplace as quickly as they could, heads down, conversation at a whisper. Everyone was eager to avoid Castor Apollonius.

Brennan began to pack up the unsold fish. 'I hope it's just for today. I don't want to have cost you your business.' The adrenaline of the near fight was fading and the possible repercussions of what he'd done were starting to set in. Once again, he'd rushed in without thinking beyond the moment.

Konstantine laughed his reassurance. 'Business might be slow for a while, but people will come around. Everyone needs fish and Castor won't stay for ever. We just have to wait him out.' He winked at Brennan and wiped a knife on his long apron. 'By "we" I mean you and me, and the village, too.'

If one thing was clear after the altercation, it was that people feared Castor's power. The fear was not Patra's alone, although hers seemed to stem from a more personal level. Captain Castor Apollonius was an intimidating man who did not hesitate to use his status—it was there in the way he dressed, in the way he carried himself. He never simply spoke, he *commanded*.

'No one likes Apollonius,' Konstantine continued. 'He may have secured our victory in the war, but it came at great cost. Many felt he made unnecessary sacrifices of our troops. Those same people fear he has come back asking for more soldiers to take on more bloodshed.'

Brennan stood up and stretched his back, looking across the market at the tavern. 'Why doesn't the village stand up to him, then?'

Konstantine paused from his chore and gave him a serious look. 'We tolerate him because we cherish our independence more than we despise Apollonius. The Filiki Eteria gave

us the cohesion, the organisation, to success-
fully rebel that previous efforts lacked. And it
worked. We have driven out the Turks, Brennan. We have some independence, but there
is a better independence to be had, one that is
not corrupted by petty chieftains. Our work
is not done. Until it is, we must tolerate a man
like Apollonius who shares our goals, if not
our ideals.'

Brennan found Konstantine's argument
humbling and shaming, too. Never in his life
had he been as committed to anything or anyone as Konstantine was to Greek independence. What was so humbling about it was
that Konstantine was a fisherman. He'd not
been educated in the great universities of the
world. He was a simple man, who lived hun-
dreds of miles from the governmental centre
of his country and yet he understood the cause.
It was something Brennan found impressive
and envious. 'Is that what he's here for? To
rally the next phase?'

'Most likely.' Konstantine nodded towards
the tavern door. 'There he is now, ready to ride
out and make the rounds.' Castor stood in the

doorway, slapping a crop against his leg impatiently as his horse was brought around, a big, black, magnificent creature. 'If we're lucky, we won't see him for a week or so. It will give you time to decide what you want to do.'

'I don't know what you mean by that,' Brennan said slowly, an uneasy pit taking up residence in his stomach. He didn't know, but he could guess.

'He's not here only for the war effort,' Konstantine said solemnly. 'He's here for Patra. He will not tolerate being the odd man out. I've told you this before.'

This was getting better and better by the moment, or worse and worse as the case might be. 'Correction, you said he was an old suitor. You never said he carried a grudge.' But he knew what Kon was implying. He had time to leave, to simply fade away before Castor came back. Maybe he should. He had meant to leave at some point anyway. Why not now before he was in the thick of trouble? 'I don't think I can decide anything until I talk to Patra.'

Brennan took off his apron. They were nearly done with packing up. 'Would you mind if I went out to see her now?' He wanted to do more than talk to her. He wanted to make sure she was all right. He'd seen her face go pale when Castor had approached. She'd been frightened and it had been a fear that went far deeper than being startled or taken by surprise.

Brennan wanted answers and he wanted them now, his impatience manifesting in long, fast strides down the dirt road away from town. Patra had slipped from the marketplace and it had taken all of his remaining patience to wait a decent interval before going after her. There'd been no question of following her directly, not with Kon's hand squeezing hard on his shoulder, cautioning him against rash action.

Patra's little homestead looked quiet, too quiet, when he approached. For a moment, Brennan thought perhaps she'd gone. But surely there hadn't been enough time for her to effect that kind of escape. A goat brayed from the tangled mess of what used to be the olive grove and Brennan knew a sense of relief. She was here.

Brennan took a step forward and heard the ominous click of a pistol being cocked. It was all the warning he had before a bullet stirred up the dust just a step ahead of him. Good lord, had she lost her mind? 'Patra! It's me, it's Brennan.' He turned in a slow circle, trying to determine her direction. 'Patra, honey, put down the gun!' A few inches closer and his Grand Tour would have come to an ignoble end in the middle of nowhere. Not that anyone would really care. But he did. He'd come out here to see if she was all right, not to be shot.

The door to her house opened slightly to test the truth of his announcement. Patra stepped out, but she did not lower the gun. That meant there must have been two. Sweet heavens, what was she doing with *two* loaded guns? But he knew. The answer was written in the dusty, tear-stained tracks that ran down her face and in the tangle of hair that now hung loose about her face having escaped its ribbon; she was giving herself a fighting chance against whatever came down that road.

There was a wildness to her, a desperation that tugged at Brennan's very core. His questions no longer mattered. They seemed petty in light of Patra wielding a gun in her home. There were only a few crimes Castor could have committed that would elicit such a response, all of them equally heinous. It no longer mattered which he'd done, only that Castor Apollonius had perpetrated them on her. That realisation forged a new kind of steel in his heart as he stood there looking at Patra, the gun wavering in her hand. He was not leaving. Leaving would be easy, but leaving would put her in the clutches of a man who embodied her worst nightmare without anyone to protect her. Brennan Carr did not want to be the sort of man who left. For the first time ever, Brennan wanted to be a man who stayed.

He took a cautious step forward. 'Put the gun down, Patra. I'm here.'

The gun lowered, slowly. 'I thought you might have been him.' Further proof that whatever had happened between her and the captain went far beyond a rejected suitor.

He took two more steps towards her. All his

instincts cautioned him to go slowly while all he wanted to do was run to her and pull her into his arms. 'You're safe. Castor rode out with saddlebags half an hour ago. He's gone.' Two more steps and he'd reach her.

He heard the hammer click down on the pistol. 'Everything will be all right, Patra.' He smiled his reassurance.

She shook her head even as relief spread over her face at his news. 'It won't be all right. He'll be back and you shouldn't be here.'

He wondered how she meant that—here at her house or here as in Kardamyli, the way Konstantine had meant it. He was getting deuced tired of people *wanting* him to leave. Brennan reached for the gun and gently pried it from her hand, laying it aside. He closed his fingers around hers and tugged her forward. 'Come and sit with me in the citrus grove and we'll talk.' He was counting on the sharp scent of the fruit, the light breeze through the leaves to calm her. Surrounded by the familiar, she might relax. He offered her a cheeky grin as they took their seats at the rough table beneath the trees. 'Now you can tell me exactly why I'm supposed to run away from Castor Apollonius.'

'You'd be foolish to stay,' Patra said, her eyes lit with a dark intensity. Brennan could feel her fingers tighten in his where their hands lay joined on the table. He'd been careful not to let her go. People talked better, said more, when they touched, and right now she needed the simple connection. 'He is dangerous. He thinks you are a spy.'

That was one for the record books. He'd have to write to Haviland and tell him. Nolan would be absolutely beside himself with laughter. Brennan felt his mouth twitch, but he suppressed it. This was no laughing matter to Patra and he would not dismiss her concerns with humour. 'I'm not a spy. Why would a spy be here?' This seemed the most unlikely of places for a spy to get any work done. What would there be to report?

'The Filiki have hopes that Britain might support a move against King Otto,' Patra explained. 'Perhaps you are here to test the possibilities. Will the peninsula rise up again? Would support make a difference?'

'Ah, the Filiki, the secret society which is not so secret,' Brennan mused. 'Your husband was part of it during the war? Were you?'

'Dimitri, yes, me only nominally. Women can't join.'

'But you helped them?' Brennan pressed, some pieces coming together. 'Apollonius thinks you might help them again?'

She shook her head. 'It is a surface-level stratagem only. He is here to investigate you. But he will stay because of me.'

'And when he learns I'm not a spy?' Brennan was feeling an enormous amount of unintended guilt. His very presence had called forth Patra's worst nightmare. But how could he have known simply being here would put her in danger?

'Then the real danger begins,' Patra said quietly. 'When he learns there is nothing you can do for him, you become expendable. He will not hesitate to kill you. He may even seek to make a martyr of you in the hopes of rallying an enraged Britain to his standard.' She pressed his hands hard. 'That is why you must go. You should be far away when he comes back.' She looked down at their hands. 'I'm afraid I didn't help any today. When he posited the spy theory, I tried to disabuse him of the idea. I didn't think it through. If he believes me, he'll conclude sooner rather than later you have no worth to him.'

'I'm pretty hard to kill,' Brennan assured her. Several angry husbands had tried over the years. He'd grown adept at knives, thanks to Nolan, an expert at swords, thanks to Haviland, and, when that failed, he could always ride like the devil, thanks to Archer. Still, this wasn't about his safety. 'I can take care of myself, Patra, and I can protect you, too.' He paused, aware that her gaze hadn't left their hands. 'Look at me, Patra. I want you to see my face when I tell you this so that you don't doubt me for a minute.' This was the critical moment, the moment she had to believe him.

She raised her eyes slowly, her gaze wary when it met his. It was the wariness that bothered him most, not because she didn't trust him. She did, as far as it went, but because he sensed the wariness was directed inward for herself. There was something she wasn't telling him, something she was holding back. 'Patra, I am not leaving you to face him alone.

I announced my intentions to court you in the fish market today. I will not run at the first sign of trouble.'

'It is only a ruse. You mean to leave any way,' she countered quietly, but he'd seen the pulse leap in her neck at his words. She had found reassurance in them despite her argument to the contrary.

'Some day, at some time in the future, not today,' Brennan said patiently. 'I will not let Apollonius harm you. Whatever happened between the two of you in the past will not happen again, not while I'm here.'

'You don't have to do this, Brennan. We made an agreement to perpetuate a short, false relationship to mutually protect ourselves from unwanted marriage overtures. You didn't bargain on this and I won't hold you to it.'

'Patra, I want to be held to it.' And he did. For her, and for him. He wasn't ready to leave Kardamyli and he'd be damned if some captain with misplaced zeal for independence was going to drive him out when there suddenly seemed to be so much to fight for. He grinned. 'Besides, I haven't finished whitewashing your house yet, or patching the shed roof. I might just have to move out here to get all the chores done.'

'You couldn't possibly! People would think something illicit was going on,' Patra protested, a good sign that perhaps she was starting to let fear release its hold.

'The people despise Apollonius. They will think I'm out here to protect you and they will approve because no one thinks a widow living alone should have to protect her home with two guns. And they'd be right,' Brennan corrected. He'd be sure to have Konstantine help spread that logic around town starting tonight. Castor might be gone a whole week or a couple of days. He wasn't about to take the chance of Castor catching Patra alone at home or anywhere.

Brennan watched her thoughts accept his reasoning and felt the tension in his own body start to relax. He arched an eyebrow and tried for some levity. He wanted to see her smile before he left to gather his things and come back. 'As for the illicit, who knows? We have a whole week, I suppose anything is possible.'

Chapter Eleven

Anything was possible. One week. Then, she'd let him go. It was an unholy bargain Patra struck with herself as Brennan disappeared down the road. She already felt lonely without him, already missed him even though he'd only be gone an hour, just long enough to gather his things and make his position clear for the gossips. It wasn't just about being lonely. She felt safer with him, too. Castor liked to work alone. He didn't want witnesses. If he came back early, he wouldn't like finding Brennan here.

It was hardly fair to Brennan. The danger increased twofold for him if he was associated intimately with her. It would give Castor another reason to hate him. She'd not been entirely open with Brennan. The danger Castor posed to him was not purely political. It was personal. Patra turned to go into the house, second-guessing herself. Perhaps she should have told Brennan all of it. Maybe, if he knew the whole horrid truth, he would be on the road out of town now instead of on the road back to her, swearing to protect a woman who didn't deserve such chivalry. But the whole truth was hard to tell because it impugned her as well as Castor. Brennan would think less of her. She was not the woman he thought she was: a virtuous, devoted widow.

She was selfish. She wanted to hold on to Brennan for as long as she could. Castor's reappearance might have cheated her out of her freedom, but it would not cheat her out of temporarily coming back to life. She didn't dare it tonight. The day had been too emotional. She had a week to enjoy Brennan before she turned him free. When she seduced him, she wanted it to be about them, just them, not about a crisis driving them together, or a release for adrenaline and fear. Tonight, she would enjoy his company at her table and try to forget the horrors of the day, of Castor's hand on her, his caress against her face. But tomorrow would be different, it would be a time to recapture the pleasures of the beach and expand on them. Tomorrow, she would take Brennan Carr to bed.

Patra tied on an apron and surveyed her kitchen. There was plenty of food for a week, even when the man in question ate like Brennan. Her decision was made. She would seize her pleasure before it was too late and she had seven days to do it. But in return for her pleasure, she would tell Brennan the truth about Castor. It was perhaps the only way to drive him off, to keep him safe. Brennan would go and she'd be alone, but that was the price to be paid. Brennan had never been hers to keep anyway.

Her efforts started at breakfast. Brennan had begun work as soon as the sun was up. This time she was ready for him. Patra had breakfast waiting, the little table set out under the cluster of citrus trees, draped in a blue-and-white checked cloth, the tray laden with bowls of yogurt and a small pitcher of thyme honey for drizzling, plates of *trikala*, the spiced sausage prepared on the peninsula, and a pitcher of goat's milk. She'd noticed how much he'd eaten that first day. Today, she was prepared. When he started into the food, she watched with relish instead of trepidation. She passed him the sausage platter. 'There's more. Eat, please.'

Brennan stuck a fork into a fat sausage. 'Why are you smiling? Is there something on my face?' He made a mock face of horror, his voice exaggerated. 'Or is there something *in* the sausage? Have you poisoned it to get rid of me?' He took a large bite.

'It's good to watch a man eat,' Patra confessed. He was going to think she was a lunatic now. But it was hard to think of 'normal' things to say when her mind was already focused on the night to come. 'It's good to cook for someone again. It's not very exciting cooking for yourself,' she added, hoping to minimise the impression that she might be just a little insane. In fact, she hardly cooked at all beyond making pita. Most of her meals consisted of pita, goat's cheese and whatever fruit she picked off her tree.

Brennan winked at her. 'You can always cook for me. I eat like a horse.' He waved his hand in dismissal when she would have protested. 'No, it's true, I do. It has something to do with how I digest food. Apparently, I burn it faster than most people.'

He finished eating and wiped his mouth with the napkin. 'Thank you, it was delicious. I could get used to a breakfast like that. I'd better get back to work before it's too hot to paint. I want to finish whitewashing the other sides of the house.'

'Are you planning on working without your shirt?' Patra enquired, gathering up the dishes.

Brennan passed her a plate, his hands lingering on hers as he stacked it with the others, a grin on his lips. 'Would you like me to?'

'I have some laundry to do today and I was noticing your shirt could use a wash. It's the least I can do for all of your help,' Patra replied coolly. She was starting to regret the offer. She'd actually meant it innocently enough, but it didn't seem so innocent now with his hands skimming hers, something she was sure he'd done on purpose. *She* was supposed to be seducing *him*. Did he guess? Surely women tried to seduce him all the time. Perhaps he was used to it.

Brennan winked. 'If you're offering, then it's the least *I* can do to oblige.' In a fluid motion he grabbed the hem of his shirt, arms crossed, and drew it up over his head. It was a pretty move that caught her staring. She nearly missed the shirt when he tossed it at her. She shouldn't be so surprised. She'd seen his bare chest in the marketplace and far more of him when they'd been swimming. And yet she thought not even a blind woman would tire of seeing him in some state of undress. Patra noticed a tiny white line low on his hip she hadn't seen before—maybe 'before' wasn't the right word. She hadn't seen it when they swam, she clarified. 'Before' implied a certain history, a certain familiarity.

She couldn't stand there and stare. She had to say something, had to prove to him that she wasn't gawking. She was a mature woman. She'd seen half-dressed men, even naked men, before. She'd seen *him* half-dressed and naked before. But all she could manage was, 'Make sure you put some lotion on sooner today. You look a little red.'

Laundry was not a good idea. Patra scrubbed at the collar of his shirt, working on a stubborn smudge. When she'd offered, she'd been unaware of how intimate doing the laundry could be—his shirt, her chemises, all lying out in the sun together drying. It might as well be an announcement of her intentions: *I mean to take you to bed*. Or maybe her imagination was overactive. She was making too much out of a simple chore.

She did not recall it being an intimate chore when she'd done Dimitri's laundry, only a necessity, one she'd taken pride in as a new bride. The way a husband looked in public reflected his wife's ability to care for him.

Patra shook out a blouse, satisfied it was clean. She draped it on a rock next to her chemise—the one she'd worn swimming— perhaps as a chaperon to prevent it from getting naughty with Brennan's shirt. Even now, a simple look at the garment raised heated memories; Brennan's hands on her, his fingers slipping beneath the chemise to touch skin, to touch her breast, then to touch lower.

Patra reached for another garment and began to scrub. What would Dimitri say about all of this? She and Dimitri had never discussed what would happen if one of them died early. In the midst of war, such talk was bad luck. No one discussed the possibility of not coming back. Would he have expected her to move on? Find another man? Or would he have expected her to remain true to their life for the entirety of hers, aside from the other risk that plagued her?

In twelve years, she'd not truly examined that question. Her grief at first had been too great and then there had simply been no reason to. The danger posed by Castor made the question irrelevant. Patra stretched her back, her gaze going to the house where Brennan's shoulder flexed in rhythmic strokes with the brush. He was beautifully made. He reminded her of a picture of David she'd seen once, a young man in his prime. She smiled to herself. Brennan was her own auburn-haired David, for a while. She watched him pause and push a strand of hair out of his face. His hair was wavy, constantly unruly, she noticed, but it glinted gloriously like red-gold in the sun.

Patra picked up her laundry basket. She had no illusions that Brennan could offer true love even in the hypothetical. For starters, he was an Englishman who'd want to go home some day. Their bargain implied it. Even in a perfect world where her secrets wouldn't come between them, there were other barriers. He was younger than she was. He would want a family at some point. He was the sort who would be great with children. She'd seen him with them at town functions and in the marketplace. He loved to swing them up on his shoulders and he always had a task for the older boys to do when they asked for work. She could see it in his laugh, with his natural playfulness. Her hand dropped involuntarily to her abdomen. She'd had a child in there once for a beautiful, short while. She might manage to have a child again, but more than one seemed unlikely at her age.

Patra reined in her thoughts. Family? Children? Where had those come from? From an impossible future, a future that didn't exist.

The week would end. There would be nothing more. There *could* be nothing more. Under no circumstances would she allow another man to die for her. She needed to be very careful she wasn't seducing herself with this domestic fantasy, just him.

That afternoon, they sat in the shade of the citrus grove, she with her mending and Brennan with his tools. He'd decided to spend the time refinishing the outdoor table. 'I'll sand it down and repaint it. It will look like new.' He'd said with a confident wink.

Patra wished she could say the same for her stitches. Brennan Carr at work on the table was proving to be distracting. She was sneaking too many peeks to sew a straight line. 'Do all English gentlemen have such excellent carpentry skills?' she asked lightly, giving up on her sewing.

Brennan snorted. 'No, hardly. It's not considered an appropriate skill for a gentleman. The mark of a gentleman is not to have to work.'

'How do you manage it, then, at home?' She

found the effortless slide of his arms nearly as mesmerising as his deboning work on the fish, as he stripped off the rough surface of the table. He did it with such ease it was obvious he'd had practice.

Brennan shook his head, but didn't break, his answer coming in rhythm with his strokes. 'I'm barely a gentleman by English standards, so people barely care what I do. My grandfather is an earl, but he had three sons, my father being the youngest. Then my father had two sons, me and my brother, and each of my father's brothers had two sons. Bottom line: that makes me the youngest of the youngest. I can claim to be the grandson of an earl, but that's all.' He gave a grunt and ran his hand over the surface, testing it for smoothness. She envied the wood.

'What does that mean, to be an earl's grandson?' She was genuinely curious now. She knew very little of English ways except for what she'd learned from the officers, but it wasn't solely a cultural curiosity that drove her as much as a personal curiosity about this man who had planted himself squarely into her life just a short time ago. Although it didn't feel like such a short while. Konstantine's party seemed a lifetime ago.

Brennan picked up a tool to help him smooth the corners. 'It means I am sent to the best schools, but no one expects me to excel. It means I get to go up to London for part of the Season to dance attendance on the débutantes, but no one expects me to marry any of them. In fact, most hope I won't because I don't have any real prospects other than my birth. I'm the gentleman who dances with everyone's cousin, but I should content myself with marrying a local squire's daughter or perhaps the daughter of landed gentry near home.'

She heard the disappointment in his voice, the bitterness that seeped in around the edges of his stories about life in England. That bitterness was somewhat surprising and unusual since he was normally cheerful. 'No wonder you're here,' Patra said softly. 'I would have left, too, if no one had expectations of me.' She saw it all clearly in the picture he painted. In England, he was meant to be a pretty ornament. No doubt he looked quite fine in his English clothes and no doubt he was a superb guest, dancing with the débutantes, flirting with the wallflowers, coaxing them to bloom with that smile of his, those eyes, that wink, his confident easy touch. But in the end, all he was meant to be was a decoration.

'I think life in Kardamyli suits you better.' It was a bold thing to say given the nature of their relationship and the nature of what would happen at the end of the week. But that didn't make it any less true. She might have only known him personally for a handful of days but she'd watched him for six months in the market. It was easy to see the life he described did not suit him.

He cocked an auburn brow at her, his blue eyes starting to dance. 'Do you know me so well, then?'

Patra raised her chin in defiance of his challenge. 'I know you're a man who needs activity, who needs to work. I can't imagine you living an idle life. I've seen you in the market throwing fish with Konstantine, playing with the children, sneaking food into widows' baskets, and I've seen you here. You can't sit still. Your body needs to be doing something. You like taking care of people, taking care of things, and you're good at it.' The guilt began to gnaw. He belonged here and she was making it impossible for him to stay.

He looked away, suddenly busy looking for a tool. Her words had touched him, she realised. The compliment made him uncomfortable. How novel, Patra thought, that the confident Brennan Carr had a vulnerable spot. Or perhaps he was unused to such compliments? It was hard to imagine the latter.

He gave up looking for the tool and leaned across the table, bracing himself with his hands on the newly smoothed surface. His gaze lingered on hers meaningfully, his eyes sparking with mischief. 'Do you know what my body wants to be doing right now?' Flirting was his coping mechanism, she realised. The compliment indeed had struck a vulnerable place.

The warm air crackled around them. Patra bit her lip in coy contemplation. 'Do I get three guesses?'

His eyes dropped to her lips. 'Do you need that many?' He held out his hand. 'Come on, I want to try out the hammock.'

Chapter Twelve

Hammocks could most definitely be habit forming, especially when Brennan Carr was in them. He had an easy air about him that made it comfortable to be in close proximity and it unnerved her just how easily she fell into that intimacy with him—and the hammock. He had them settled in short order, her head tucked in the crook of his shoulder, his arm about her, the weight of his body setting the hammock to a gentle rocking motion. To lie here like this, with him, so close, so intimate, held a sense of rightness, like it had on the beach, proving that it indeed seemed natural to be with him. Nothing had seemed like this since…well, just since. She was used to dividing time and experience into life with

Dimitri and life after, but she didn't want to make that comparison today.

Beyond them, the house gleamed sharp blue and white in the afternoon sun. It looked better than it had in years. 'I always meant to get to the whitewash,' Patra began. Perhaps he wondered why she had let the place go. 'I never got around to it. The first few years, the house didn't look so bad and I put it off. Then, something always got in the way. There was bread to bake, clothes to wash, soap to make, something in the village that needed doing. But I'd waited too long and it was no longer the simple task of just a single coat. It was so dirty it would require more work than I could do.' For various reasons. It was more work than she could do on her own and more work than she could allow a man to do, more interest than she could allow a man to show in her for fear it would bring down Castor's wrath. But those were things she couldn't tell him today.

'You don't have to explain.' Brennan shifted his body slightly in the hammock as if he were uncomfortable with the intended praise. 'It needed doing and I did it, case closed. I think I'll start on the olive grove next. Tell me about it, what do you do with it? How much does it produce?'

'It depends. Every other year is a big harvest. That's standard for olive crops. All of us in Kardamyli are on different cycles so the village as a whole always has a strong crop even if some individuals have a smaller yield that year. I forget where my crop is at. The last three years, I've just foraged in the near trees for whatever I needed.' Patra winced as she thought of how tangled and overrun the grove would be. 'It will be a mess up there. I have only five acres up on the hill that backs the house.' Was he thinking of Katerina Stefanos with her enormous acres and regretting his decision?

'Five acres is plenty if you're not an olive farmer.' Brennan gave her absolution.

'My husband was a fisherman like Konstantine,' Patra told him. 'The olive grove was mostly just for our personal needs and for me. I made soaps to sell and trade in the market.' She had liked doing that, liked the idea of making her own money to contribute to their little household, liked being able to buy herself an occasional luxury or a small gift for Dimitri. But her financial freedom had died with him. These days, whatever she could make and trade was her sole source of income. It was enough for food, but not much else, certainly not luxuries like a length of lace to decorate a plain chemise.

'Once the olive grove is functional, you could do that again.' Brennan interjected himself almost directly into her thoughts.

If she could keep it up. Patra feared that Brennan's efforts would simply go to waste once he left and wasn't there to maintain them. She didn't want his work to be useless. He was giving her small property a second chance. Perhaps if she were careful, she could maintain it. Maybe there was a younger boy in the village who could help her, someone who wouldn't rouse Castor's wrath.

Brennan's hand moved along her jaw, his thumb at her lip, making her pulse speed up. 'Stop thinking, Patra. Hammocks weren't made for it.'

A light breeze filtered through the grove, cool against her face. It made her indolent and bold. 'What were they made for, in your opinion?'

Brennan angled himself up carefully on his arm and leaned towards her, his eyes playful. 'For this.' His mouth took hers in a summer-soft kiss, his hand resting warm and steadying on her midriff. Oh, yes, this was definitely going to be habit forming.

Warning to self: dinner in citrus groves could be habit forming. Actually, there was no 'could' about it. Brennan was pretty sure it was. There was no question of it when he stepped around from the side of the house where he'd washed up and sniffed the air, catching the scent of *trikala*. Patra's back was to him as she set down the last dishes. Brennan smiled to himself, watching her work. She'd taken an extra effort with her appearance tonight. Her hair was been pinned up in a special braid and she wore an embroidered blouse and skirt he hadn't seen before. *For him.*

He wasn't sure of the last time a woman

had dressed especially for him. Had there ever been? There were some whores in Paris who had *undressed* for him, but it wasn't nearly the same. A woman in London dressed for herself, dressed to compete with the other women, or dressed to show off her husband's or father's wealth. But Patra had voluntarily dressed for him. The gesture was unsuspectingly touching and personal.

'Dinner smells delicious.' Brennan strode towards the table. 'Is there anything I can bring out?' She had worked all day, too, and yet she'd prepared this meal, another personal touch. There was no cook, no scullery crew to do this work.

Patra turned and smiled at him, her eyes taking stock of his appearance. Brennan felt his shoulders square, felt himself stand taller, wanting to do the freshly laundered shirt justice. 'Everything is on, just come and sit.' She stood aside, revealing their newly reclaimed table in the citrus grove and all its bounty. It was covered in a white cloth, a thick candle protected by a glass chimney stood in its centre surrounded by summer dishes: a salad of romaine and artichokes, tomatoes and olives; a bowl of hummus; a small platter of *trikala* left over from breakfast and a basket of warm pita. A pitcher of wine stood at the ready near durable pottery goblets—other than the linen cloth, there was no fancy china or crystal here.

London might scoff at the simple food, but Brennan thought it was perfect. Who wanted hot, heavy food when it was so warm? Salads, vegetables and bread were ideal for the climate and there was plenty of them. Patra poured the wine as he sat, handing him a goblet, and he felt like a king. 'I wish I could capture this in a picture,' Brennan complimented. 'The food, the setting, it's all beautiful.' He let his voice linger over the last to imply she was included in that.

'If the setting is beautiful, it is because of you.' Patra gestured to the grounds. 'You have painted my house.' She raised her goblet. 'We should toast to your good health because I can probably find more projects for you to do.'

Brennan gave a mock groan, but his mind was already whirring with a list of 'nexts'. 'Tomorrow, I'll do the roof of the goat shed.

That way, they can stay out of the olive grove.' He knocked his goblet against hers. 'Cheers.' It was good to make plans and he didn't need to be a genius to realise it was novel, too. He wasn't usually a plan maker. In London, he had drifted aimlessly from activity to activity.

Brennan filled a plate for Patra and then saw to his own. 'How is it you are so good at fixing things if it's not a gentleman's standard accomplishment?' she asked, sipping from her wine glass, waiting patiently for him to finish piling his plate before she began to eat.

'My family's home is three hundred years old.' Brennan dipped a slice of pita into the thick hummus. 'It hasn't been ours for the entire three hundred years, but that doesn't change the age. Old houses need help. There's always a shutter to nail on, a chimney to re-brick.'

He could see Patra's mind working through the logistics of the statement and coming to the obvious conclusion. 'Aren't there servants who handle that kind of work?'

'Sometimes. But even then, my father doesn't notice everything that needs to be done.' It was the lesser of two evils to admit when compared to showing off his family's sporadic tendency towards financial insolvency. Repairs cost money and his father had purchased a property beyond his means to sustain adequately. The house had been an impulse buy on his father's part, one of many impulse buys, such as the racehorse that now lived a life of luxury in their back pasture after his father realised he couldn't ride the beast. The Carrs weren't poor, but they often lived beyond their means in ways that stretched their funds. His father was never concerned about where 'more' would come from, it would simply come. Eventually. Even if it meant selling a painting or two while waiting.

'Your father's not a carpenter, then, not like you?' Patra refilled his glass.

'No, he's not,' Brennan said, taking an extra-large mouthful of salad, perhaps on purpose to avoid the expectation to say more. It wasn't always comfortable to talk about his father. But Patra wouldn't let him off that easy.

'Just no?' she cajoled with one of her teasing smiles. 'What's your father like? Is he like you?'

That was just it. Was he? Brennan slowly spread another piece of pita with hummus, his words a carefully formed thought spoken out loud. 'I don't know. Maybe he is, or maybe he was like me once and he isn't any more.' He glanced at Patra. She was watching him, waiting for him, patient. 'Here in Greece, family is everything, one is judged by who his family is.' It was true in England, too, but less intensely if you weren't high-born to the peerage and Brennan wasn't so high born.

'And you don't want your family to be the measure of you?' Patra finished the thought for him.

Brennan nodded slowly. 'I want you, I want anyone I meet, to judge me on my merits. I want my successes, my shortcomings, to be mine alone.' This was the demon that had chased him across a continent. He'd never given it words before, it had always been a niggling suspicion, an unnamed, amorphous thing that lurked in the dark places of his mind, something he held at bay with women and wine and one party after another. He'd come to Europe to find himself and up until now, all he'd really managed to do was run from that self. It was a rather sobering realisation.

'You've been gone two years, do you miss them?' Patra asked.

Did he? 'Perhaps a little.' Brennan leaned forward. 'It's not that I don't like my family. My mother laughs and sings all day. She likes to arrange flowers so the house is full of fresh-cut bouquets. At any given moment, one faces the risk of running into my father stealing a kiss and sometimes more from her in any given room of the house. They married young and they're still fabulously infatuated with one another, some might say to the point of silliness.' He gave a wry grin and caught Patra smiling.

'What's so wrong with that?'

Brennan wrinkled his brow and blew out a breath. 'They didn't save much of that fabulous infatuation for their children, that's what's wrong with that. My brother and I sort of grew up on our own. There wasn't much discipline in our house. We went through tutors like that.' Brennan snapped his fingers. 'We'd skip out on lessons to go swimming and when the tutor complained to our father, our father would merely laugh and say, "Boys will be boys."'

Patra gave him a sly look. 'I would think a great many boys would love a father like that.'

'I suppose, in the short run. But boys need discipline and structure, too, they need a father to be stern when warranted. My father just wanted to be a friend. When I left on my trip, there was no farewell party. It was almost as though the family had forgotten I was leaving that day. At the last minute, my father called me into his office, only I wasn't alone because my friend, Nolan, was with me.' Brennan gave a self-deprecating laugh. 'This is rather embarrassing, I shouldn't be telling you. You know what, I'm not going to tell you, forget I brought it up.'

Patra raised her dark brows in encouragement. 'Oh, no, you don't, you cannot start a story like that and then back out. You have to tell me.' She held up the wine bottle to assess how much was left. 'You can have the rest if you tell me,' she bribed.

Brennan smiled and hung his head. It was hard to refuse her when she looked at him like that. 'All right, you drive a hard bargain, but remember you've been warned. My father called me in and I was thinking, *At last he'll say he loves me, he'll tell me how much he'll miss me, how he can hardly wait until I come back*. But, no. Instead, he passed me a package of French letters and said, "Don't get syphilis."'

'French letters?' Patra enquired.

'Condoms,' Brennan explained, watching heated recognition dawn on Patra's cheeks. He started talking a little faster to ease the moment, to ease his guilt. He should have gone with his gut instinct and not told the story. 'It's sort of humorous, but in England we call them French letters, as if the French were the ones wicked enough to make such things. But in France, they call them *les capotes anglaises*, English caps, because only the English would be so debauched.' Brennan laughed an apology. 'I'm sorry, I should not have told you. It's not an appropriate story.'

Patra reached out a hand and covered his where it lay on the table. 'But it is, in its own way,' she said softly, eyes shining. 'I want to know about you.'

It was about the most potent thing she could have said to him. She wanted to know him and it was nearly his undoing. When had anyone wanted to know about Brennan Carr, youngest son of a youngest son of an earl? Brennan looked at their hands joined together. Usually, it was he who initiated any contact. Having that role reversed was...validating. It made him suddenly shy. He searched his mind for something funny, clever to say to take the edge off the moment. 'Well, now you know what happens to boys who are left to grow up wild. They end up in fishing villages on the Peloponnesian Peninsula.'

'Is that good or bad? Are we too simple for your tastes?' Patra asked laughingly with a smile, but he sensed his answer mattered to her, that something important hinged on his response. Still, he would make his answer honest.

'Yes, it's a very good thing.' Brennan held her gaze, bringing his hand up to lace his fingers with hers. 'I'm closer to life here, the way I want to be.' He tried to explain, tried to give words to thoughts he'd formed over the last six months. 'Here, our tables are filled with food that is grown, raised or caught by our own hands and then prepared by those hands. The clothes we wear are sewn by those hands. Every day is filled with purpose.' Brennan shook his head. 'I've been here six months. I thought I would have been ready to move on by now, but I'm not. This is where I want to be.' A shadow passed over Patra's face and he shrugged his shoulders with a laugh. 'You think I'm crazy, don't you? Am I making any sense?'

'I don't think you're crazy at all. Chores are not just chores, they're gifts we give to one another. There is purpose *and* honour in that. It removes the drudgery of it,' Patra answered, saying much more eloquently what he'd tried to express.

Brennan smiled, watching the candlelight play across her features, letting the night and the wine work its magic. Perhaps he had imagined the shadow. 'You *do* understand. I knew you would.' The words came out husky, as he was overcome with sudden emotion. In that moment he knew one truth: he wanted her. Not just as an extension of this Greek fantasy he'd called to life with his words, but for herself. Patra Tspiras understood more than the ideas he'd shared. She understood *him* in a fundamental way no one else ever had.

Chapter Thirteen

She understood all too well and that was the peril of it. He was making too much sense, raising too much guilt. In a week this *affaire* would be over and his dream would be gone, another man's life ruined because of her. *He* would trade his world of relative privilege for this if he could.

The very thought conjured dangerous ideas, stirred flickers of hope where there shouldn't be any. What if she'd met this man under different circumstances? What if there wasn't a threat to his life? What if there was no ruse? What if they were truly free to pursue this relationship to its natural outcome? Patra rose and began gathering the plates on to a tray, trying to dislodge the growing fantasy. The *what if* game was far too hazardous to play. She picked up the now-empty wine bottle. 'Shall I get another when I go in?'

Brennan rose and joined her, his hands taking the tray from her, his voice full of quiet, husky authority, pushing them gently towards the evening's outcome. 'Let's go in together.'

It was a good thing she wasn't holding the tray without help. She might have dropped it—and yet this was what the entire evening, the entire day had been moving towards. It was what she'd decided she'd wanted. But her body still reacted with an unprecedented amount of excitement. She took a deep breath, trying to get herself under control. She wasn't a school girl with her first beau. She could do better than this.

She made him wait in a bid to get herself under control. It was legitimate at first. The food needed to be stored and the dishes needed to be soaked at the very least. But Brennan managed to make even the most mundane chores into foreplay with nothing more than his eyes. His gaze followed her, watching her hands rinse the dishes, watching her stretch up to put the dishes in a high cupboard, watching her bend to toss out the dishwater, his gaze letting her know he appreciated each curve, each turn of her body. Dishes had never been so sensual. She reached for a kettle and his hands closed around hers, setting the kettle aside. She was conscious of his body warm behind her, his voice at her ear.

'Enough. We won't need anything else tonight. You are stalling, Patra. Shall I go?' He was making her ask for it, as she'd known he would. He had made the parameters of their association clear from the start: nothing would happen she didn't choose. He'd enforced those parameters at the beach and now he was enforcing them again. His hands tightened over hers, the only sign of his apprehension that perhaps she might deny them both at the last.

He was right, of course, she *was* stalling, but not for the reason he thought. The exact opposite, in fact. She summoned the courage to say the words out loud. She turned in his embrace, her arms going about his neck. 'It's just that I want you more than I realised and I fear it has quite overwhelmed me.' *I don't want to disappoint you. I haven't done this in a long time and never with a man not my husband.* Would he hear the rest of it in the unspoken words?

His hands framed her face, his mouth taking hers in a slow kiss that reminded her of all that had moved them towards this consummation. This was not a randomly made decision. The kiss was meant to prove the rightness of her choice. They would not disappoint each other, they couldn't. They already knew pleasure was possible between them, but his words were meant to absolve any lingering insecurities. 'It's a first time for me, too, Patra.' He kissed her again, his tongue lingering on her lips, tasting of dinner's wine. He *knew* how hard this was for her—this decision to move beyond what her life had become. His next words, murmured against the column of her throat, seemed to understand that.

'Come to bed, Patra, I want to make love to you.'

It was a potent invitation, full of reverence, full of promise, and it swept away her remaining thoughts of inadequacy or latent remorse.

'And *I* want to make love to you.' Patra slipped her hand beneath his *foustanella*, sliding it up his thigh until it cupped the warm, rising length of him. She heard his sharp intake of breath as her hand came around him, felt him swell as she whispered. Brennan kissed her hard then, drawing her against him, letting her body feel the efforts of her words, the fire in his blood, of his desire being permitted free rein at last.

She gave a laughing gasp as her feet left the floor. Brennan swept her into his arms, laughing with her as he navigated the short distance to the bedroom. He set her down on the bed, but when she reached for him, wanting to pull him down beside her, he stepped beyond her reach with a whispered admonition. 'Not yet.'

He lit the lamp beside the bed and stepped into its glow, his hands already pulling his shirt over his head. 'First, watch me, *look* at me.'

How could she not? His presence permeated all her senses—the sight of him, bare-chested in the lamp light; the smell of him, all soap and man lingering on her clothes; the taste of his tongue in her mouth; the husky drawl of his voice as he gave his command: *look at me*.

He was gorgeous, something she already technically knew. It wasn't the first time she'd seen him bare-chested, it wasn't even the first time she'd seen him naked. She understood his choice of words better now. She was to look at him, really look. There was no running towards the waves, no bright afternoon sun or list of chores, there was nothing to interfere with her gaze, nothing to limit her to furtively stolen glances. She was to look her fill, to engage the intimacy of gazing to its fullest.

He stripped off the belt of his *foustanella* and set it aside, his voice drawling a private history lesson. 'Hindu worship involves the *darshan*, the two-way vision in which you and the god behold one another... Hindus believe the eyes are the gateways to one's soul. To honour that, men and women avoid direct eye contact in public, even husbands and wives reserve such intimacy for private times.'

Patra's hands clenched in the bedsheets as she fought a wave of desire. Just the sound of his voice, that low private drawl, the feel of his eyes on her, watching her watching him, was nearly enough on its own to bring her to climax. Brennan's hands rested on the waist of his *foustanella* for a long moment. He let it drop in one swift motion and then he was naked before her, unabashedly, thoroughly, gloriously naked, and it was spectacular not only in its completeness, but in its stillness.

Patra let her eyes start at the full curve of shoulder, bulked with muscle, let her eyes drift to the planes and ridges of his chest and follow them down to where they tapered to the flat of his stomach—the square bone structure of the male pelvis subtly drawing the eye lower to the auburn thatch of hair that housed his phallus, proud and rigid under her stare. It was matched by the power of the thighs that framed it, legs muscled from walking, hiking, riding, running. This was the body of an outdoorsman, a man who spent his days in pursuit not only of sport but of labour, a man who knew how to harness the power of his body, and had.

Patra swallowed hard, desire rising. He'd used his body for her in labour, tonight he would use that body for her pleasure. She rose from the bed, moving towards him, her fingertips trailing down his chest, wanting to touch the marble smoothness of it, the rough contours of his muscles. He was the work of the ancient masters brought to life. She held his eyes, letting him see her pleasure, letting him know how much he pleased her, letting him know, too, that she understood the other message: now, it was her turn.

She gave him a gentle shove, pushing him into the room's single chair, and stepped back. She let the light fall over her, through her, let it create shadows and hollows with her linen. Sometimes the most provocative things were the things that were frustratingly obscured. Brennan crossed one leg over a knee, his gaze dark and glittering as it met hers. His desire made her brave, obliterated any modesty that might have remained. She wanted to please him as he had pleased her.

Patra slipped the drawstring of her blouse loose and lifted it over her head, her breasts pressing against the thin linen of her chemise. She felt Brennan's eyes on her, felt her nipples tighten in response to that gaze until the linen they brushed against became a source of rough arousal. Her skirt followed, joining Brennan's *foustanella* on the floor, and she was bare to him, the dark triangle between her thighs visible beneath the hem of her chemise. Brennan was silent.

Patra planted a foot on his knee and arched her leg prettily. She reached for the pins in her hair, pulling down the braid and letting it fall over one shoulder. Brennan took a sharp breath. She licked her lips and flashed him a coy smile. 'Perhaps you prefer your London ladies with more? Stripping is not an elaborate affair. Here, we don't have silk stockings to roll down, or petticoats to take off.'

'No, ah, this is fine. Quite fine.' Brennan managed a hoarse, stammered response.

'Perhaps, if I took this off, too…' Patra raised her arms and slid off the chemise, tossing it to the floor. 'Does that *help*?'

'*You* are a vixen,' Brennan growled, but he claimed retaliation, placing a strategic kiss up high on her inner thigh, reminding her that they were both naked now, exposed not only in the physical sense, but the emotional, too. His hand ran up the leg she'd perched on his knee, his eyes gleaming dark cobalt. He made her feel beautiful, perfect, when he looked at her that way. His thumb grazed the seam of her furrow. She sucked in her breath.

'I am the only woman in the world when you touch me like that.'

'You are. You are the only one that matters because you're mine.' Brennan drew her down to his lap, taking her astride him. She could feel his phallus pressing between them. It would be nothing to take him inside right here on the chair, but he had other ideas. He wanted to look, wanted to touch and she hadn't the will to argue; not when his hand slid up past her ribs to cup the soft underside of her breast; not when his head bent and his mouth closed over her nipple; not when her body felt so very alive with each new touch. This was a sweet heaven, a tantalising but bearable pleasure, feeding the slow fire within her. His hands were at her back and she arched against them, her breasts thrusting forward, begging for his mouth, her desire rising—it would not be bearable much longer.

'Put your legs around me.' Brennan lifted her, his hands cupping her buttocks as he carried her, at last, to the bed and followed her down, his arms bracketing her head, taking his weight as his body fitted itself to hers, to the welcoming space between her thighs.

Patra wrapped her arms around his neck, pulling him to her. She was not fragile, he needn't be afraid of breaking her. Their kisses were hungry, heated, rougher than the earlier ones. Want was driving them both hard now that their bodies sensed the wait was nearly over. She could feel him ready himself, his body making a slight adjustment, his phallus at the edge of her entrance. He would find her ready.

Brennan thrust, her body stretched and accommodated. He thrust again and she took him in full, revelling in the slide of him in the tight, moist walls of her channel. This was what she was made for, what life was made for. A gasping moan escaped her as he sheathed himself in her again. She'd forgotten, but that was where any comparison ended. Her body arched as she picked up the rhythm of Brennan's lovemaking, her body and mind recognising this desire, this fever, was not merely a replacement for what she'd shared so many times with Dimitri. This new rush was entirely unique to the heat between her and Brennan, and it went straight to the core of her, a hot, white bolt every time he moved inside her until that bolt became a hot sheet of heat from which there was no momentary relief, nor did she want one.

She wanted the heat, wanted the pleasure of its torture to overcome her until she could do nothing but...scream... Was that sound her? It came again in raspy, sobbing gasps of over-whelming release and another cry mingled with it, this one male; husky, panting groans in shaky intervals as Brennan's arms trembled about her, taking her in his embrace. She clung to him, her legs wrapped tight around him, holding him tight with every muscle her body possessed as he emptied himself.

It took an age for the shattering heat to ebb and Patra was in no hurry for it to subside.

She would have lingered longer in its warm, residual tide if she could, the feeling of peace, of completion, indescribable. Here, nothing mattered. In this space, they were free. Brennan's head rested on her breast, his breathing falling into a steady, sleepy pattern. Patra ran her hand through his unruly hair, marvelling at his ability to fall asleep so automatically. He wouldn't sleep for long. She knew from their afternoon spent in the hammock that he'd wake up shortly and be fully charged. If only it were that easy. If only there was nothing that mattered but this room and what they could do in this bed. If only she could hold the dawn at bay. Then she wouldn't have to face any of the realities that waited for her.

'Patra?' Brennan murmured, his breath warm against her breast. 'You're thinking.'

'You're awake already.'

'I've been awake. I could feel you playing with my hair and I wanted to enjoy it.' Brennan chuckled, the sound of it vibrating soft against her chest. It was a warm sound, a comforting sound. 'But you're not thinking about my hair.'

'No, I'm thinking about this,' she lied, sliding her hand beneath the covers to his phallus and feeling it pulse to life. Far better to do this than to waste her time in regrets. There would be enough time for that later. He gave her a wicked smile and pulled her atop him with a lazy drawl, his hands settling on her hips. 'You said you wanted to make love to me, here's your chance.'

She took that chance, sliding confidently down on his phallus, already roused and primed from her hand. She rode him slowly, focusing on his pleasure, on the dark-cobalt flames of his eyes when she cupped her breasts, lifting them high and running her thumbs over them, the sharp intake of his breath when she ran her hands down her body and in between his legs, and again when her nails grazed the vulnerable inner skin of his groin.

'Zeus have mercy!' Brennan bucked, his head back, his hands gripping her hips tight as she moved on him. She loved seeing him like this, loved knowing that he wanted to lose himself in this thrill, a thrill she could give him, and perhaps a thrill *only* she could give him. He groaned, the pleasure-pain moan of climax sweeping towards him as he thrust with her. This was not a game for him, but something unique, and it intoxicated her. He wanted this with her, wanted to lose himself with her and that was perhaps the most glorious of compliments, to share this intimacy together. He lost himself then, his body pulsing its confirmation, and maybe for a few moments she lost herself, too, to hopes, possibilities and improbabilities.

Chapter Fourteen

The captain wasn't going to like this. Castor Apollonius's secretary slipped from his hiding spot in the hillside and stretched his cramped limbs. He'd waited an extra half hour just in case the Englishman had come out of the house. The Englishman hadn't. He didn't expect the man would. As to what the Englishman was up to in there, the conclusion was obvious, even if he hadn't witnessed (which he had) the long romantic dinner in prelude. There were only so many reasons a man went into a woman's home this hour of night.

Whatever else the Englishman might be, he was definitely in bed with the captain's lady. The two of them were bold indeed. The Englishman had barely waited after Castor had left town before hotfooting it out to her place. The secretary chuckled. For the Englishman's sake, he hoped the sex was worth it because there would be hell to pay when the captain got back. Perhaps Patra Tspiras had forgotten what fear felt like, or what happened to those who displeased the captain. He would send out his report immediately with a rider in the morning. Once the captain heard the news, he would likely come back early.

The secretary pulled a small notebook from his pocket and took out a stubby pencil to jot down a few reminders. When it came to Patra Tspiras, the captain would want details.

The devil was in the details. Brennan moaned and stretched in the morning sun, his arm reaching across an empty pillow. That was detail number one. Patra was already up and moving. He could hear her in the other room. That was a first for him. He *never* slept the entire night with a lover. *He* was the first one up, the first one gone. It avoided messy aftermaths.

That he hadn't been this morning was further proof as to how extraordinary the night had been. Their lovemaking had been more than a physical release; a part of him had not wanted to escape the aftermath and what it might mean. Never had he worked so hard, or waited so long, to seduce a woman as he'd waited for Patra Tspiras. He'd once talked a woman into bed within five minutes of meeting her. Compared to the days he'd laboured here, the latter seemed an eternity.

Now that it had happened, the comparison to other *affaires* seemed inept. This was no seduction. Seduction implied some sort of game, it required strategies and manoeuvres, none of which were truly in play here. What had occurred between him and Patra had been entirely natural and it was entirely new territory for him. He'd not lied when he'd said it would be a first for him, too. He was used to whores and courtesans with their tricks, bold women of the *ton* who had their own games they liked to play with a willing young man who gave them back their youth for a night. But not virtuous widows who loved with contemplation, with honour, for whom this act meant something more than physical pleasure and yet there had been an expectation of that, too. Hence detail number two: the aftermath. Domestic tranquillity.

The clatter of pans and the spicy scent of *trikala* met him as he swung out of bed and padded towards the basin and pitcher of washing water. Brennan poured water and lathered his face with soap. This was the simple dream, wasn't it? Waking up to a meaningful day of work, hearing the comforting sounds of a breakfast being prepared? In his shiftless years among the *ton*, this was the intimacy he'd hungered for. It was no wonder his *affaires* had left him empty. He brought the razor down the side of his cheek, slicing through stubble, wishing he could slice through the thoughts in his mind as easily. If this was what he'd unconsciously been seeking, what did it mean? Now that he'd found it, what did he do about it?

Was it merely the life in Kardamyli that satisfied him or was it something more? Was it Patra who satisfied him? And how could he know such a thing in the span of so little time? It was easier to believe it was Kardamyli that pleased him. He'd been here long enough to know that. But Patra? All logic told him it was too soon to know. A few days, a magical night in her arms, did not warrant a lifetime. And yet, weren't the tales of his friends evidence to the contrary? Evidence that the *coup de foudre* existed?

Brennan finished washing and reached for his clothes. They had been carefully laid out for him on the chair, another detail that demanded his attention, a reminder of what it felt like to be cared for *and* cared about. It was a simple, thoughtful gesture, made personally for him. It was not the act of a paid valet who cared only for his salary. Patra had picked his clothes up from the floor where he'd let them fall last night and laid them out. The gesture mattered. Such personalised thoughtfulness mattered.

Brennan thrust his arms through his shirtsleeves and pulled it over his head. What would Patra say if she knew what he was thinking? An imaginary line had been crossed. He couldn't pretend sex had just been sex. The stronger realisation, though, was that he didn't want to pretend. His very thoughts were a clear violation of their agreement—to use one another to avoid permanent entanglements. Between last night and the episode with Castor in the marketplace, the ruse was becoming decidedly real.

Brennan fastened his *foustanella* around his hips. Was that why Patra was up early? Why she hadn't remained in bed? He understood too well the urge to want to flee the bed when things got too close. Had that propelled her out of bed this morning? Had she, too, realised a line had been crossed and even now was grappling with her response? Would she, like him, be willing to go forward with the line behind them, or would she demand they retreat back to the safety of the ruse where nothing was as it seemed?

She had a lot at stake—her fear of Castor to overcome, her reputation in the village to preserve. He understood those were significant things to risk on a young stranger who had so little to offer her beyond himself. But she was not the only one with something at stake. For the first time, Brennan felt nervous over what a woman's response might be. But that didn't mean he wasn't willing to fight for it. Already, a campaign was forming in his mind. There wasn't a woman yet he couldn't win. He wasn't going to stop now.

Brennan stepped out into the main room of the house. Before last night, he'd never been inside. His time here had been conducted out of doors. Most of Greek life was. Houses were small, made for coolness and shelter, but not for gathering, not like English town houses with their drawing rooms and ballrooms that could accommodate two hundred, and dining rooms that could seat twenty-four. The inside was neat and well kept, clearly bearing the brunt of her housekeeping efforts. Patra turned from the cooking, a tray in her hands loaded with his new breakfast favourites, *trikala* and honey-drizzled yogurt, a smile on her face. Time for phase one of his campaign. He favoured her with a dazzling grin as he took the tray. 'What shall we do today?'

It had taken some effort to talk Patra into having a day off, but by the end of breakfast,

Brennan had convinced her to take a walk into the hills. They would be alone, away from the reminders of her worries. She had packed a lunch basket and he had slung it over his arm as they set off. It was cooler higher in the hills and there were some ruins Brennan had wanted to see. Patra knew them and she gave him a history lesson as they hiked the distance.

'This is the area that we call Old Kardamyli. We live closer to the sea now, but it wasn't always possible or safe. In the hills, it's easier to see who might be coming and it's easier to defend,' she explained. 'Two hundred years ago, this part of the peninsula was overrun with bandits and crime. Wealthy families would build stone towers to protect an area.' She shot him a sly look. 'Of course, those families weren't doing it purely out of altruism. If you wanted the protection of the tower, you had to pay for it in tithes and allegiance.'

They came to the stone tower and Brennan was surprised to see it was more than a tower, but actually a jail and a church; St Spyridon,

Patra lectured, as they stepped inside the cool, dark interior.

'St Spyridon? I've never heard of him.' Brennan laughed. 'He doesn't have a very popular name. I can't imagine children being named Spyridon, not like Matthew or James or Peter.'

Patra gave him a friendly punch in the arm. 'That's because you English have such a limited imagination when it comes to names. Peter, James, bah! What plain names when you could have Agfayah or Ambrus.'

'Or Spyridon. It sounds too much like spider.' Brennan gave an exaggerated shudder. 'Of which I am sure there are plenty in here.'

Patra laughed. 'Not scared, are we? It is an *abandoned* church. What did you expect? As for Spyridon, you might rethink your attitude about him. He was a wonder-worker in the third century. The stories of the saints tell he used his earthly goods for the benefit of those around him, even the homeless. God gave him his ability to heal in exchange for his selflessness. There are other stories, too, about the people he healed.'

They came to a ledge hewn into the church wall and Brennan stopped to sit. He pulled Patra down beside him. 'I think this proves how useless Oxford really is. I spent four years there and never learned about Spyridon or the stone towers.' There was a lot he hadn't learned in college.

'What is Oxford?' Patra asked.

'A university in England that gentlemen send their sons to. We're supposed to be finishing our education there, but everyone knows we're not. It's a pretty open secret. We spend more time drinking and wenching.' Brennan sighed. 'I tried, I really did, but I couldn't stick with any subject long enough.'

'Why do they send you if they know you're not studying?'

'To get us out of the way, I suppose. Better to make trouble far from home than at home where they have to deal with us. Better to let the deans clean up our messes,' Brennan joked. 'I always felt it was more true in my case. My parents were far too eager to get rid of me.' Patra didn't laugh.

'And this "Grand Tour" you're on? Is it

meant to be educational, too?' she asked quietly in the dimness of the church.

'Yes, it's supposed to introduce us to new cultures and political systems so we're prepared to take up our roles in the diplomatic corps or our seats in the House of Lords if we're heirs.' Brennan blew out a breath. 'Of course, those are not situations I'll be offered.' He could only imagine how many wars he might inadvertently start as a diplomat, instead of stop. He could hardly see himself spending hours poring over the words of treaties or sitting through tedious negotiations. He'd rather be throwing fishing nets with Kon.

Patra's hand stole over his. 'Why did you come, then?'

'You don't want to know.' Haviland and Archer had come for legitimate reasons, as part of their station in life. But he and Nolan had been escaping the shadow of scandal yet again. It was hardly anything to brag about. It would definitely not impress Patra or prove to her he was a reliable sort, certainly not after the story he'd told her at dinner.

'Now I absolutely do. You can't say that

and not tell me.' She paused, maybe rethinking the wisdom of her protest, maybe imagining all the bad things he could have done. He had to tell her.

'I was my friend's second in a duel. Duelling is illegal, but we did it anyway. *He* did it, technically. But I was his second, so when it was decided that all would be forgiven if Nolan just went abroad for a while to let everything cool down, I went with him.'

'Was it over a woman?' Patra breathed, clearly caught up in the romance of a duel.

'No.' Brennan laughed. 'I'm sorry to ruin it for you. It was over a dirty accusation at cards. A viscount's son accused Nolan of cheating and Nolan's honour could not let the lie stand.' He remembered that night in striking clarity. Haviland and Archer had left the club. The viscount's son would never have made the accusation in front of them and their bloodlines. But Nolan and Brennan didn't have the status, they could be provoked. 'My friend has this talent, it's a gift really—like Spyridon's wonder-working.' He winked at Patra. 'He can count cards. He never loses.'

She would be disappointed in him. It had been a stupid duel for a stupid reason. But her next words surprised him. 'Of course you went with him, even though you didn't have to. You're loyal, you said so yourself. It's the same reason you came after Castor for me.'

Maybe it was the dimness and the quiet coolness that was acting on him, maybe it was her words and the absolution they carried. In London everyone saw him as the man most likely to sin. But she saw him as the most likely to save. Brennan leaned near her ear, his voice low. 'I *will* be loyal to you, Patra. I give you my word. I promise.' God, how he wanted her, right here in the church, this beautiful woman who saw the best in him. He would have promised her anything to have her.

He wanted last night again, to see if it could be repeated. He'd felt physical pleasure himself on countless occasions, that great draining sensation of becoming utterly empty. He placed a kiss in the soft spot between her neck and the lobe of her ear, his hand skimming her ribs, issuing an implicit request. She gently pushed him away. 'Not here,' she admonished.

'But somewhere else, perhaps?' He nuzzled her neck, feeling her pulse rise beneath his lips. With Patra, the sex was different, it had been not so much about emptying himself, but about being completed. He had not been alone at the end. He usually saw to the woman's pleasure first. Last night it had been mutual, seeing to one another's pleasure together. She'd been there with him, not before him.

She laughed her acquiescence, a deep throaty sound. 'You are persistence itself.'

Brennan put an arm about her waist and led her out of the church, into the sunlight. '*You* require it.' But he was no Spyridon. He would win no awards for sainthood. He wasn't nearly selfless enough. Outside, they found a grassy patch shaded from the sun in a corner of the tower ruins. Brennan shook out their blanket. 'This is the best I can do.'

Patra moved into him, pushing him back on the blanket, and straddled him. 'The best you can do? I shall be very disappointed if that's true.' She slid a hand up his *foustanella*, finding him rising and ready. She gave a wickedly flirty smile. 'I see that you lie, sir.'

* * *

This was an intoxicating, dangerous game she played with herself. Last night had become a slippery slope to more pleasure. It would make the end more difficult when it came— and it *would* come. Five more days remained of this fantasy at best and she wanted to make the most of them. There was something she could give him in the interim, something that might make up for what she'd cost him in the end. He couldn't and wouldn't love her, not when this was over. But maybe she could help him love himself.

Brennan's confession in the church had made her ache even though he'd couched it in humorous remarks about English education. She'd seen the real tragedy beneath the words. This handsome, charming man didn't know or understand his true worth. And she railed silently at the family who had taught him such doubt. She wanted to teach him differently. Patra pushed his shirt up, running her hand over his torso. 'I don't think I mentioned how handsome you looked in the market the other day.' She bent over him, making a kissing trail up his chest. 'I like the throwing-fish act.'

Brennan grinned. 'Is that all it takes to entertain you? A shirtless man throwing fish?' He was putting himself down again. She was starting to see his humour in a different light.

'Well, not *any* shirtless man,' she prevaricated playfully, drawing a nail back down the kissing trail and feeling him shudder. She could hardly confess more at this stage of their relationship, which was awkwardly both existent and non-existent. She might acknowledge to herself that the line between pretence and reality was a bit blurry at times, but she never wanted *him* to suspect it. For starters, it wasn't part of the ruse, but the ruse was beginning to matter less with Castor's reappearance in her life. What mattered now was that he believed she wanted him to leave. 'Oh, I'm not picky. It doesn't have to be fish. It could be a shirtless man repairing my table, painting my house, pruning my bushes. I am looking forward to that.'

'Pruning your bushes?' Brennan laughed. 'I'll show you pruning your bushes, you wicked girl.' He seized her about the waist and flipped her on to her back. She gasped her surprise as he burrowed beneath her skirts, throwing them up in the wake of his hands. It was wildly erotic to be bare beneath the sun, to feel Brennan's laughing breath against her curls. But that was nothing compared to the feel of his mouth on her, his tongue at her furrow, licking her essence. This was an exquisite, intimate enjoyment that had her arching against his mouth, crying up to the sky as he moved from furrow to pearl, his tongue flicking against the tiny nub. She pounded a fist into the ground, helpless against the wave of pleasure that swept her.

She gave in to it, letting it take her away, knowing it was merely a prelude. Before she'd even recovered, Brennan levered himself over her, thrusting deep, starting the pleasure all over again, this time for them both.

'How's that for pruning?' he managed at her ear, his words coming ragged and hard as he thrust again.

'I, um, think…' Speech was hard, so very hard at the moment. 'You are quite the gar-

dener, Brennan Carr.' Then words and the
ability to make them suddenly became un-
important for a long while.

Chapter Fifteen

'I love Greece.' Brennan lay on his back, staring up at the sky while she drew idle designs on his chest. Patra thought she might love these moments afterwards as much as she loved the moments that brought them to this point of replete togetherness, when all seemed right with the world because the world was just the two of them. It was an exciting and yet dangerous way to feel. It made her feel young again, innocent again. And it was impossible to sustain.

'I've never been some place where the sun shines so much,' Brennan mused. 'In England, the winter lasts for ever. The spring is full of mud and rain until May. Then, when heat does come it makes the city miserable and you have to wear full gentleman's attire—coat, shirt, waistcoat and cravat—and pretend you aren't sweltering.'

Brennan shuddered and she laughed. 'No wonder the *foustanella* appeals to you so much.'

'It's not just the weather,' Brennan confessed. 'It's the food, there's a freshness to it, a zest. English food is bland, Patra, and heavy. It's the whole life. I can work hard here...' He paused and she watched a thoughtful expression cross his face as he searched for the right phrase. 'I am *myself*. I've been looking for the place where I could be me.' He smiled up to the sky. 'I've finally found it. I had to travel across Europe to do it.'

He was about to lose it. The guilt began to prickle again. She ought to tell him now, but how could she when he looked so happy, so at rest? She'd gone into the ruse under the assumption that he would leave Kardamyli some day. There had been no rush until Castor had shown up. But Castor's arrival changed everything. Now, in order to protect him, she had to force him to leave earlier than he would choose. More than that, she was forcing him to give up his dream for her, something he had not bargained on.

Brennan sat up suddenly and rummaged in a pocket inside his waistband. 'I almost forgot, I have something for you.' He held up a length of bright blue ribbon and the tempting *what ifs* began to rise once more: what if he didn't leave? What if he chose to stay indefinitely? There was hope and horror in that prospect for her. To stay would last only as long as Castor allowed it. Castor would extract his revenge; next week, next month, next year. The waiting for it would become another level of his torture.

'For me?' She smiled, trying to ignore the tightness in her throat, the sting of tears in her eyes over the simple gift.

'I saw it in the market one day. I thought of you. You've been wearing your hair down, lately.' It was ridiculous to feel so moved by a strip of silk. But it had been so long since she'd had a gift that was entirely luxurious, entirely selfish. She couldn't eat a ribbon, she could only wear it, only be pretty in it—something she hadn't been able to risk.

'May I?' Brennan reached around her. She felt his hands skim the nape of her neck, gathering her hair, felt his fingers firmly tie the ribbon and then linger at her shoulders. 'Blue becomes you,' he whispered. 'You should wear colours more often.' But colours weren't practical and colours called attention to the one who wore them. One more price she'd chosen to pay for anonymity.

Shadows were starting to fall, a signal the afternoon was fading and, with it, their time together. Brennan took her hand as they started down the path. She liked the feel of his touch far too much. She'd started this ruse to keep herself safe and it might have achieved that in terms of keeping her out of her friends' matchmaking line of fire if Castor had not returned. But who would keep her safe from Brennan, who made her feel alive with his broad smile, his laughing eyes, his wicked mouth and that body made for sin? She'd not bargained on such a thorough reaction to him. Things had spiralled wildly out of control where Brennan was concerned. When all of this had started, she'd been mentally prepared to lose him. She hadn't been prepared to love him.

Patra was distracted. She had been since the ruins. Even now as she prepared the evening meal, her hands were clumsy. She dropped the knife and sloshed the wine, refusing to take any help when he offered.

Brennan didn't need Nolan's gift of perception to know Castor Apollonius was the likely source of her preoccupation. But he didn't fully know why. Oh, he was starting to. Puzzle pieces were beginning to fall into place. The ribbon had nearly made her cry, a reaction he hadn't expected. It was a simple gift. Coupled with what Konstantine had shared with him, it told him volumes. This was a woman who had *chosen* to live a life of quiet self-deprivation since the death of her husband. She had let her home outwardly fall into disrepair rather than take help from the village men. She had eschewed any level of personal luxury for herself, as well. He'd seen the clean but mended quality of her undergarments and shifts. It was as if she'd wanted to make herself as unobtrusive as possible. Until he came along.

That was the other conundrum. He understood why she'd agreed to his ruse. It helped preserve her anonymity, it took her away from legitimate, real social relationships. But no matter what she'd intended to get out of their arrangement, she'd come alive for him, and now she wanted to retreat. Now that Castor had come along. Her past and her present had collided and it scared the hell out of her. Why?

It was time to find out. He'd seen the quiet stoic woman she'd been in the marketplace months before. That woman hadn't been happy. But the woman who had danced in his arms beneath the stars, the woman who had roused so thoroughly to his lovemaking, was a happy woman in those moments. He didn't want to lose her, not now when he'd just found her, not now when she had just found herself. If he could do just one thing right, one thing that mattered, he wanted it to be this. Patra Tspiras deserved to be redeemed.

Outside, they set the table in the grove together, laying out dishes of olives and tomatoes, goat's cheese and hummus, wine and bread. Patra tried to light their candle and burned her fingers on the match. Brennan took the matches from her and laid them aside. He would get no better opening than this. 'I think we need to talk before you burn something more than your fingers.'

Patra sat down and gave him a wary look. 'Talk about what?' She was going to make him work for her confession.

Brennan didn't back down. He held her gaze steadily. 'What it is that has you distracted: Castor Apollonius. Tell me about the war, Patra. Tell me about your husband and how he died.'

She baulked with a pretty smile. 'Why does it matter? It's all in the past. It can't be changed.' Her hand slid invitingly to his leg. She was going to seduce him into forgetting his questions. Brennan recognised the manoeuvre. He'd used it often enough in the past to avoid unpleasantness. He covered her hand where it rested on his thigh.

'To defeat one's past, one has to face it,' Brennan said quietly, firmly. 'But you don't have to face it alone. I'm here and I want to know what happened between you and Castor. The village believed he was going to marry you, sweep you off to a life of riches and prestige. They believe, too, that you cried off for political reasons. I think it was more than that.' He squeezed her hand. 'Patra, Castor will return. If you want to protect me, you have to tell me. What caused a passionate woman to retreat from her community, to retreat from life?'

For all of her efforts to fade into anonymity, it had finally happened. Castor Apollonius had come back for her. Brennan had a right to know why. It was his life that was in danger. She withdrew her hand and folded both hands on the table. She couldn't bear to feel the moment when he became repulsed. She held his blue gaze, so full of genuine concern. It might be the last time he looked at her like that. She wanted to savour it, remember it. 'I will tell you,' she said slowly. 'But you will hate me for it when I'm finished.'

He shook his head, wanting to voice a protest. She cut him off. 'You don't know what I have done.'

She started at the beginning, painting a picture for him of life during the war, of how Castor's organisation, the Filiki Eteria, had brought real hope to the cause for the first time, of how Dimitri had joined the brotherhood, as had others in the village and throughout the Peloponnese. Everyone was full of patriotic fire, wanting to do their part for independence. There had been meetings and plans. There was optimism. This time things would be different.

'I was caught up in it, too. As a young girl, I'd listened to my parents tell tales of failed rebellions in the northern provinces. As I grew older, I understood these rebellions were isolated incidents, individual groups who couldn't hope to succeed for long against the mighty Ottoman Empire. When Dimitri and I married, the Filiki were on the move to change that. They were organising Greeks spread throughout the empire. This time there was a co-ordinated effort, the Ottomans would be forced to fight on multiple fronts. The Greeks would become like the many-headed hydra of myth.'

She could hear the pride rising in her voice as she recounted the early days. 'It worked. The Peloponnese had risen up. Those days of victory were heady. But in retrospect, I see now that the victory had been a bit overestimated. The Turkish troops had seceded most of the Peloponnese not because they were outgunned by our efforts, but because their resources were all focused on the mainland against Ali Pasha. But it was victory and the Filiki used it to raise more troops, to fight more battles in the hopes that one of the Great Powers—Britain or France or Russia—would see our ability to win and come to our aid.

'That had been in 1821. In 1822, we were still waiting and still dying for the cause as Turks fought to retake the Peloponnese.' Patra remembered those bloody days, days spent worrying over Dimitri who was travelling with the fighting force, days of worry that if the army fell, what would the Turks do in retribution when they came to the village? The Turks at Tripolis had been massacred. 'Our great fear was that they would come here wanting revenge, if they could get here.

'That was when we met Castor. Morale was flagging. The Filiki sent him to raise our spirits.' Castor Apollonius had been the military leader of the corps in this part of the peninsula. He'd been a handsome, patriotic firebrand of a man, full of charisma and persuasive skill. His presence had been reassuring in those difficult days, reassuring to *her*. He was also passionately devoted to the Filiki Eteria and he inspired that passionate devotion in others as well, even when the war dragged on and it became clear that blind devotion to the Filiki was misplaced. 'My husband was away fighting. I clung to Castor's reassurances desperately. I regret ever thinking that fervent patriotism was synonymous with human goodness.

'By 1823, one thing was clear: the Great Powers were only going to aid in moderation now that victory seemed inevitable. Some British came as a result of the Filiki's efforts and the efforts of Greek clubs in London. But they only came independently, as private citizens who wanted to help the cause like your English poet, Byron, or military men who lent a hand training troops out on the Ionian Isles. The French came later, helping to sweep away the Turks at Modon, but too late to make much difference for Dimitri.' The telling became more difficult here. She could no longer talk just about the war, just about facts.

'Your husband fell at Modon,' Brennan encouraged gently.

She had to be strong and go forward. She would not be the death of one more man who had the misfortune to care for her. Patra gathered her control. 'He was killed and it was all my fault. By then, I had known Castor for three years. I thought Castor was my friend, *our* friend. He had Dimitri transferred to his regiment "to keep him safe", he assured me. I was unaware Castor's feelings ran far deeper and far differently than mine.'

She watched Brennan's face, knowing the moment he understood her meaning fully. She could see waves of emotions roll through Brennan; there was the righteous anger of chivalry, of wanting to protect her from such injustice. She felt his question before he asked it.

'How can you be certain of such a thing?' She didn't blame him for asking. It was not doubt that drove the question, it was incredulity. What sort of man did such a thing?

'Do you know the story of David and Bathsheba, the one from the Bible?' Her lips had suddenly gone dry, her throat squeezed. She'd never told anyone this. Would Brennan believe her? Would it matter if he didn't? If he thought she was a lunatic, it would be enough to drive him off and that was what she wanted.

Brennan's own voice was hoarse, his mind making awful connections. She could hear it in the strain behind his words. 'King David puts her husband on the front line of battle where he knows the man will be killed.'

'That's how I know.' Her voice was hushed in the darkness. 'That's why I fear for you. He's made it very plain if he can't have me no one will, not even my husband.'

Chapter Sixteen

Good God, Apollonius was a murderer *and* a psychotic bastard. Brennan was glad he wasn't standing. He would have been reeling. Apollonius had used the veneer of patriotism and friendship to set up a murder, to steal another man's wife. The last part gave Brennan chills. A man wanted him dead.

It wasn't the first time a man had wanted him dead over a woman, but it was the first time it had been articulated with such cold-blooded premeditation. Usually, when he was chased down by angry husbands, et cetera, it was very much in the 'heat of the moment'. If those men had succeeded, they would certainly have regretted their actions by light of day. Apollonius was not a man who had regrets. If he wanted a man dead, he'd already justified it to his soul.

Brennan watched Patra. She was waiting for a response, waiting for him to hate her, to think she'd played the harlot in her husband's demise. He wanted to leave the table, change locations so they could begin a new conversation. He rose and held out his hand as he'd done the night before. 'Come walk with me.'

He could feel the tension in her body as she took his hand, her touch wary. He still hadn't responded to her revelation. What did one say after learning of their own murder attempt? What did one say to a woman who had lived with the knowledge of her husband's murderer all these years? Heaven help the man, him in this case, who had to respond to *both*. There was no comfort he could give that would be adequate. He took refuge in a question. 'Why didn't you tell someone?' But he knew the answer before she voiced it.

'Who would believe me? There was, there *is*, no proof. Men die during battle. Modon was no different, in many ways it was worse. A *lot* of men died there. Why should Dimitri have been any different than any other soldier who fell? People would say my grief made me desperate, that it made me willing to lash out at any convenient thing or person in an attempt to blame someone for my loss. It is what grieving people do, after all.'

And Apollonius had made himself very convenient. *Everyone had thought he would marry her, that grief had brought them together.* Apollonius and she had already been close thanks to the war. Brennan felt his gut clench with something primal and possessive. He could imagine Apollonius setting himself up as the close friend of the deceased and the deceased's widow. He could imagine Apollonius holding her as she sobbed, offering words of comfort, telling her how her husband had died a warrior's death, how he'd been with Dimitri at the last, probably at great risk to himself, making himself out to be a hero in the débâcle. Brennan could imagine punching Apollonius in the face for such treachery. His fist clenched involuntarily. He'd make sure he got his chance. 'Apollonius is a vile bastard. I am sorry, Patra.'

They reached the hammock, a scene of more pleasant memories, and Brennan wanted to invoke those memories now to hold back her darkness and guilt. He got on first and stretched out before pulling her down beside him. It felt good to hold her, to be able to offer her comfort. But he was aware gentle caresses and words like *sorry* were not nearly enough. They did not make up for the years she'd gone without smiling, gone without dancing, without socialising, not only because no one would believe her about Apollonius's scheme, but because she was protecting the cause. Apollonius was the village's link to independence, to the great cause their men had died for, a cause they believed in. What had Konstantine told him? They loved independence more than they hated Apollonius? Patra had protected the cause all along, keeping it pure in the minds of the town, at great expense to herself.

'You should hate me, Brennan. I've put you in danger.' She sighed against him.

'I don't hate you. It's not your fault. The fault is entirely Castor's.' Brennan realised something else, too, as they lay together in the hammock, now that the truth was between them at last. 'Is it just me Apollonius wants to kill or is it any man who gets close to you?'

'Any man,' Patra whispered, as if a quieter voice made the disclosure less dangerous. 'He told me so himself.'

It explained so much. Why she clung to the guise of devoted widow for years beyond her required mourning, why she refused her friends' efforts to see her marry. She had made herself as inconspicuous as possible. Even her home had become inconspicuous. She'd refused the villagers' help because that help would have been male. It would have risked drawing Apollonius's attention to the men who helped her. Perhaps the fall into disrepair had been somewhat calculated. She'd been protecting everyone, not just the cause. Until he'd come along and ruined everything.

Brennan shut his eyes tight against the guilt. What a fool he had been. 'I didn't understand.' His words were inadequate. It wasn't so much his possible murder that haunted him now, but his hand in what he'd done to her. She had been safe, free of trouble until he'd started painting walls, thatching sheds and using her to escape the parson's mousetrap. He'd drawn Apollonius's attention to her with his stupid ruse. 'I have to make this right for you, Patra.' He had no idea how to do that but he would find a way. It wasn't fair for her to suffer because of his foolishness.

'Why do you have to make it right?'

'None of this would have happened if I'd let you be. You were willing to dance with me, but nothing more.' He could see why now. Hindsight was brilliantly, blindingly, painfully clear. She had known what would happen. She'd tried to warn him. 'This is all my fault.'

His fault? How did he reason that? Patra levered up carefully on one arm, the hammock swinging from her efforts. 'How can it be your fault, when it's all *mine*?' She was the one who had drawn Castor's attention in the first place and caused Dimitri's death. She had known what would happen if she encouraged Brennan's attentions, false or otherwise. She was the one who had argued herself into believing that she could steal a bit of happiness, that Castor would never find out. She'd *known* what sort of fire she was playing with. 'I knew. I should never have accepted your offer.' Except then she would have never known this. These last days, swimming at the beach, none of it would ever have existed. Their eyes held and she waited to see the recrimination in them. Surely, he would hate her now for dragging him into this.

The recrimination didn't come. She had to try harder. 'I *seduced* you, last night in fact, after we knew Castor was here.' Surely that would incriminate her. But it only made him laugh. So much for trying harder.

'I seduced you, too. I would say we're fairly even on that score. You started it last night, but I get credit for the swimming, St Spyridon's and at least for part of last night. I get credit for this, too.' He kissed her slowly then, his mouth lingering on hers, calling up once more the warm, sweet heat that gathered in her belly, and pushing her fears aside for something far better. She couldn't give in. Not yet. She couldn't let him brush this off, couldn't let him pretend this didn't matter. She had to have his word that he would leave.

'Brennan,' she murmured between kisses, 'Apollonius will see you dead. We can't ignore him.'

She felt his lips turn up into a smile where they pressed against hers. He laughed against her mouth, a warm chuckle. 'Then I want to be sure I die happy.'

'You have to be serious.' But she already knew she was fighting a losing battle. Brennan had miraculously managed to move over her without upsetting the hammock. 'Have you ever made love in a hammock?' he whispered against her ear, a hand sliding beneath her skirts.

'No, have you?' Her thoughts were still on the other conversation, the one they needed to have.

He laughed down at her, his eyes sparking. 'No. I don't even know if it's possible, but we're going to find out.' He moved too quickly and she gave a yelp, part-laughter, part-scream, as the hammock rocked dangerously. 'All right, rule number one: everything happens slowly.' Brennan laughed, letting the hammock settle before he moved again.

Everything did happen slowly, which was as much torment as it was treat. Making love in a hammock was definitely an art form. 'I think it would be easier naked,' Brennan teased, sliding into her with a sigh. 'Ah, at last.' In the rising heat of their desire, it had seemed to take an age to get her skirts up.

But 'at last' was merely a prelude to another kind of waiting. The torture-treat wasn't nearly over. Brennan was meticulous with his strokes; sliding in deep, only to pull back in a deliberate retreat through her slick channel and slide in again until her body was more than ready to remind her she had not had her pleasure tonight. And, oh, how that pleasure built. He knew where to slide, where the most responsive parts of her channel would quiver with sensation as he slid past. She fought the urge to buck, to rock against him. Such a motion would definitely overset the hammock and see them on the ground. But the inability to do so only added to her rising need for release.

'Please, Brennan!' she urged with her words

what her body dared not. Her hands knotted in the mesh of the hammock, every muscle straining in the effort to stay still. She was almost there. She wanted two, maybe three hard, fast thrusts and this delicious torture would be over.

Brennan flashed her a sinful grin, knowing full well he was the source of her agony and her ecstasy. One wicked word hovered on his lips. 'Wait.' She risked pummelling him with a fist but he was too fast. He pinned her wrists, drawing them slowly up over her head, his breathing starting to come in hard pants that punctuated his words. 'I. Wouldn't. Want. To. End. Up. On the ground. Just now.'

And, in truth, neither did she. She stilled as he came into her one final time and she knew the wait was worth it. This was not relief, or even release. This was *rapture.* Every fibre of her body felt his muscles tense and relax, tense and relax as his release pulsed, as he poured life into her. Maybe it moved her so intensely because she recognised the danger he was in and she knew, deep her in heart, the end was very near.

Brennan collapsed against her, his skin

faintly sweaty. 'Ah, now we know. It's possible.' He pressed a kiss to her shoulder. 'The lengths I go to for science.' She wanted to laugh with him, but her thoughts were far darker than his. It would kill her to lose him, to lose his laughter, the light he brought to each day. She hadn't realised how dark her days had become until he'd burst upon them. Well, she had survived darkness before. She would survive it again. Only this time, she was much more aware that surviving wasn't living.

She reached up a hand to push all that untidy auburn hair back from his face. She wanted to be able to see him when she asked him, 'A man wants you dead. Doesn't that bother you?'

He gave her the impish half grin that brought the village women to their knees. 'It does, but I refuse to obsess about it. I'd rather think of the silver lining.'

'Oh? What would that be?'

'It adds to the authenticity of my courtship. Surely I must be sincere in my attentions if Apollonius wants me dead.'

She wouldn't let him laugh it off this time. She held his face between her hands as if that would make him more serious, as if that would stop him from smiling. 'Brennan, why don't you hate me for this?'

Brennan sobered. She could feel the muscles of his face letting his smile fade. He lifted himself from her, very carefully. Her body stilled, her breath caught. He was beautiful and primal in this moment, his body taut with intention. Whatever he was about to say was more important than anything he'd ever said to her. 'Patra, look at me. I want you to see me when I say this because I have never said it to another woman before.' There was no boyishness about him now. He was all man. The warrior in him frightened her and thrilled her. 'The reason I don't hate you is because I'm too busy loving you.'

She stared at him, stunned. The words took her like a blow to the stomach. It was the best she'd hoped to hear and the very worst. 'How can you possibly love me?' Time had been too short. She'd done a terrible thing to him. There were so many reasons to argue. But Brennan put a finger to her lips.

'Hush. A man knows these things.' Brennan swallowed, his throat working obviously, a sign of what this confession had cost him. 'I love you. That's all that matters. You don't have to say the words for the sake of good form. I'm not asking for reciprocity. You don't have to love me, but *I* love *you.*'

But he wanted it, might crave it even. She could see it in his eyes. She thought of St Spyridon's when he'd told her about his parents. How there hadn't been enough love to go around once they'd been done loving each other. She saw him clear by the light of the moon. That was his mission, his gift: to spread love, to let people know there *was* enough love. No one need be left out. And maybe, just maybe, after giving all that love, someone, somewhere, would give a little back. To him.

She wanted to be the one to do it. No matter how foolish, no matter what the cost. Castor Apollonius and his threats could go hang. Whatever happened, he would have that. 'I want to say them.' Her voice was hoarse, her throat a little dry. His blue eyes darted away from her. 'No, now it's your turn to look at me.' Strength returned to her tone. 'I want you to see me when I say it.' She used his words against him, and his eyes slowly, hesitantly returned to her.

'I love you, Brennan Carr. I love your spontaneity, I love how you eat piles of food, how you make every ordinary day an adventure. I love how I feel with you, like I'm alive again, like anything is possible…' she paused and smiled '…like making love in a hammock. I love your heart, your kindness. I saw you give Widow Anastas the extra fish.' She thought he blushed. '*I* love *you*.' And she did. She loved him enough to give him up. Wasn't that what love was all about? Self-sacrifice for another?

'You forgot to mention my body. You love my body,' he joked. She would have swatted him for insouciance, but it was his way of coping with the intimacy of feelings put into words, something he wasn't familiar with. She wished she could make sure he became comfortable with such a thing, but that required him being comfortable with himself and the idea that he was worthy of love. Such acceptance took time. She doubted she would have that much time. She would not have him long enough.

She laughed. 'And I love your body.' She

ran her hands up his arms, revelling in their corded length, their strength. 'I would like nothing more right now than to have that body carry me into the house and make love to me in a proper bed.'

'Mmm…' Brennan bit her neck. 'Why don't we stay here and do the hammock again?'

'I don't think I can survive it.'

Brennan slid a hand underneath her blouse. 'You'll survive it because this time we'll both be naked.'

She smiled, moving her arms to help him with her clothes. 'Why not?' Once more into pleasure's breach she slid because she didn't know when she might get the chance again. He loved her and she loved him. They'd said powerful words to one another. But those words didn't change the situation they faced or what she had to do. If anything, they made it more imperative. Another man who loved her wasn't going to die for her. When Castor returned, she'd go straight to the devil himself and bargain for Brennan's life with her very soul if need be.

Chapter Seventeen

Castor looked at the report. It was official. He hated the Englishman. Hated him enough to interrupt his circuit of the coastal towns to come back to Kardamyli and send out the invitations to his banquet two days earlier than planned. It had taken a day and a half of hard riding to return, but he couldn't stay away knowing every day he did was another day the Englishman was in Patra's bed, filling her head with ideas of freedom, making her forget who she belonged to.

Castor crumpled the report with a vicious fist. He hated the Englishman for more reasons than his possession of Patra. The Englishman was to be envied. He commanded the village's affections. People *liked* Carr. His secretary's report had held more details than merely the salacious ones of what had gone on at Patra's house. The men liked drinking with Carr, the women insisted on buying his fish. Konstantine Zabros's business had never been better. He made people smile. People would follow him if he ever understood his own power.

Leaders recognised other leaders and Brennan Carr was definitely a leader. That made him dangerous to Castor. Castor was honest with himself. The people of Kardamyli followed him these days out of fear, not out of a sense of fealty. He wished it could be otherwise. He recognised fear had limitations. It wore off if it wasn't exercised and regularly proven. It appeared Patra was proof of that. For four years, he'd stayed away, confident that she was his, confident that she'd learned her lesson about drawing men to her. He'd been busy in Athens, focused on his political advancement with the new king, and the last suitor, a farmer from a neighbouring village who had barely shown interest, had been easily chased away.

He had been certain all he had to do was wait for Patra to recognise he would be her only option, ever. He'd been wrong. While he had been building a future for her, for them, among the elite in Athens, she'd taken an Englishman to bed, thinking it was safe to do so, forgetting she belonged to Castor. It would be best for all parties involved if Brennan Carr simply disappeared. Castor fingered a sharp letter opener. He'd kill Carr if he had to, but as a foreign national, Carr's death might come back to haunt him. He'd rather just have Carr leave. He glanced at the clock on the table-turned-desk in his makeshift office. It was nearly ten o'clock. The banquet was tonight and he rather thought he'd see Patra come through his door any moment. He knew what made her tick. She would want to 'save' Brennan.

The thought made him laugh. She might understand how he operated, but she still made the same faulty assumption about dealing with him. She assumed because she played by the rules, he did, too. He wondered what she'd bring to barter. He might even take what she offered. But that wouldn't change the outcome. He'd do whatever he wanted to do in the end, bargain or not.

His secretary stepped into the office, a figure in skirts following behind him. 'You have an appointment, Captain. Widow Tspiras has requested an audience.'

He looked up with a smile. 'What a pleasant surprise and right on time, too.' He loved it when his machinations came together. 'Well, well, well, Patra. I see you have come to beg.'

Patra had known exactly where to find him. Wherever Castor went, he had a personality that was larger than life, that filled every room, attracted every eye. It was what made him such a charismatic patriot for the Greek cause. He was handsome and immaculate, always, even in the morning. No one would guess he possessed such dark sins beneath all that perfection. Once upon a time, even she hadn't guessed. How could she expect others to when he was a consummate master of his masquerade?

She hated that she was so predictable. He'd known she was coming. He'd known the invitation would bring her running. 'Come sit and eat, Patra. There is fresh coffee and *bougatsa*.'

He waved towards a small table and two chairs where the pastries were laid out. 'I remember how much you like them. Do you still have a sweet tooth?' He winked as if they were old friends, as if there was no spilled blood between them. She wanted to slap him.

'I prefer to stand and I am not hungry,' she bit out tersely.

He made a *moue* of disappointment. 'I had them prepared especially for you.' Her temper rose at his audacity. He'd been *that* certain she'd come.

'Are you sure? I can't possibly eat in front of a lady.' If that were true, it would be one of the few things he wouldn't deign to do in front of a lady and certainly not the worst. If he was waiting for her to give him permission, she wouldn't do it. It was a petty battle, but she was not about to condone even the simplest of his behaviours.

'I came to tell you to leave Brennan Carr alone.'

Castor gave a cold laugh. 'You came to *tell* me? Not to *ask* me? My, my, Patra. You've grown bold or else he must mean a great deal to you.' Castor's brown eyes glinted dangerously.

'I came to *tell* you because he means nothing to me. He means nothing to you. He is not a spy. He is not part of the cause. He merely stumbled upon the village and decided to stay. That is all. He is innocent.' This was the lie she had to sell. If he was convinced Brennan was nothing to her, he would leave Brennan alone.

Castor made a great show out of smoothing the crumpled papers. 'After reading the details of my secretary's report, I must disagree with that particular assessment. It appears you have a great deal of affection for him. I admit to having some curiosity about the depth of those affections. He is so much younger than you, after all.' Good lord, what was in that report? Patra felt a cold sinking feeling. He'd had her watched! She decided to brazen it out.

'You can't go killing every man who does a chore around my place. He fixed my shed and painted my house.' Patra held his cold stare with a steely gaze of her own. The last accusation angered him.

'He did far more than patch a roof. I have

it all right here, if you care to read it? Perhaps you might remember this: "They sat at an outdoor table for supper, with candles, before rising and going into the house *together* around eleven o'clock. The Englishman did not come out again." Does that sound familiar?' He shook the papers at her, jealous rage starting to brew. Patra swallowed hard as he came around the desk. She could see the flare of his nostrils, but she refused to flinch. She had a knife. She would use it, she reminded herself, if he came closer, if he tried to touch her.

As quickly as the rage had come, it was gone, replaced by sadness. He stopped in front of her, just out of reach. 'How dare you treat me like this, Patra? How dare you make me the villain in the sad drama of your life? You still blame me for Dimitri all those years ago. I did not kill him! He died, like soldiers do.'

'Because you arranged it! You put him in the thick of the battle. I saw the battle reports. I talked to the other captains. Everyone said you ordered his unit into the thick of the fighting knowing full well they would be annihilated,' Patra fired back, less intimidated by him in her anger.

'I saw him die, yes. I held him in my arms at the end.' Castor stepped forward, stalking her now, his voice silky. She moved to the other side of the pastry table, keeping the furniture between them. 'Shall I remind you of his last words? He said, "Look after Patra...take care of her for me." Your husband *gave* you to me and yet you defy me at every turn.' Something raw and covetous flashed in his eyes. 'You defy him, too, by denying his dying wishes. He *wanted* us to be together.'

Patra's hand closed over the hilt of her little knife. She had heard that story before. Her response was still the same. 'So you say. Why should I believe you? There is no proof those were his last words or that you were even with him. Of course he would have asked that, he thought you were his friend.' She preferred it that way. She did not want Dimitri to have died knowing he was betrayed.

Castor stopped stalking. He held his arms out to his side in a gesture of reconciliation. 'Patra, you know there is nothing I wouldn't do for you. I have wealth, a home, servants. Once the Filiki regains their political power, I will have even more and social standing to go with it. We could be one of the greatest couples in the new Greece, a new state we wrested from the hands of the Turks. This has always been our dream, why do you baulk now?'

Patra narrowed her eyes. He chuckled. 'You dislike having your sins revisited, I see. But it's no sin that you roused to me once. I would have made an honest woman of you, I still would.'

'I did not rouse to you. I did nothing disgraceful with you.' She spat. But he was right. Even though she'd never acted on it, there'd been a time in the early days after Dimitri's death before she knew what Castor had done, when she had thought she hungered for him. He had been handsome and consoling, so very eager to comfort her at a time when the loneliness had threatened to swamp her.

'Now there is this Englishman.' Castor was watching her. She held her face still, willing it to blankness. She refused to be intimidated by him or the memories, but she'd forgotten how commanding he could be, how intuitive. He knew how to play on a person's fears.

He picked up a pastry and extended it to her. 'You say he is nothing. If so, eat this cream puff. Prove to me he is nothing.'

What ridiculous game did he play now? She was sure he played one. What did one bite prove to him? What did she risk by not doing it? What did it cost her beyond her pride? Surely she could afford a little pride if it protected Brennan. Patra reached for the pastry, but he raised it, holding it out of reach.

'No, Patra. I will hold it while you take a bite.' He was going to make her pride *suffer*, she could hear it in his tone, deceptively silky, hiding the malice beneath. But she knew it was there. 'Come, take the food from my hand.'

She wanted to refuse, wanted to grab the pastry from him and smash it into his face. He knew it, too. She hesitated, her pride getting the better of her in the moment. Perhaps this was what he wanted. He wanted her to refuse so he could blame her for forcing his hand. Brennan would not die for the lack of a bite. Patra gathered her pride and bit into the pastry, her teeth sinking into the creamy interior. She tried not to think of his hand holding it, or of what she was doing.

Castor wasn't going to let her off that easy. His eyes watched her chew, watched her swallow. 'Do you remember how I fed you when you were sick, how I took care of you before you lost the baby?' His tones were soft now, conjuring up one painful memory after another. 'Do you ever think about that, Patra? About why that happened?' He forced another bite on her. 'Everything happens for a reason. With Dimitri gone, only the baby stood in our way of making a fresh start. Then it, too, was gone. I took care of everything for you, for us.'

Patra choked, gagging on the cream. It was the one thought she had never allowed herself to entertain—that Castor had been responsible for the miscarriage. It wasn't because she wanted to protect Castor, she was far beyond that. She wanted to protect herself. There was only so much tragedy a soul could bear. Losing Dimitri and the baby so close together had been all she could take. It was easier to believe she'd lost the baby due to grief. It was what the doctors had believed and it made logical sense. No one wanted to believe a man would be depraved enough to kill a woman's husband and her unborn child. She fought back the rising bile. She would not retch in front of him. He would relish the degradation, would relish the victory in knowing she had to face that truth.

'Just one more bite, Patra,' he said, as if she hadn't just choked on the last. 'Take it for your Englishman. It's rather intimate, isn't it? Eating out of someone's hand?' he drawled, his voice low. 'This pastry, this cream, your mouth on it, your teeth sinking in to it, it all calls to mind another rather intimate act you might perform for me with your mouth.'

Patra spat the remainder of the pastry into his face, anger taking hold before she could think better of it. He'd deprived her of so much and she wanted him to pay. Cream and spittle clung to his cheek. 'I would never do that!'

He withdrew a handkerchief from a pocket and wiped his face, unfazed by her outburst. 'I think you would do a great number of things if you thought it would keep your Englishman safe.' A malevolent grin twitched at his lips. 'After all, you ate the pastry.'

She began to argue, to protest, but he overrode her with his voice. 'The Patra I knew would not have eaten the pastry. She would have fought me because she had nothing left to lose. But you...' his gaze raked her intimately '...you, come in here glowing and radiant, quite obviously the products of a night well spent in a lover's arms, and ask clemency for him. You, my dear, are a woman who has *everything* to lose. It makes you vulnerable. You ate the pastry and you will do a sight more than that if you think it will keep Brennan Carr alive.'

'I hate you.'

'I'm sure you do, despite my willingness to kill for you. If that is not devotion, I don't know what it is. Many women would see that as a grand token of affection. But in a gesture of good will, I will make you a deal. You did do my bidding, after all, as much it galls you to admit.' He chuckled and rested a hip on the table. 'Brennan Carr is to be gone in two days. Either you see to his exodus, or I will.' He picked up a *bougatsa* and bit into it. 'Don't look so horrified. I'm not asking you to kill him. Just make him leave.' He took another bite, his tongue licking the cream off his lips. 'Of course, *I* might, but I hope it doesn't come to that.'

Her knife wouldn't be enough. She couldn't carve out Castor's heart with its small blade, but she did think about it. 'That is no deal at all. You are forcing me to give him up!' It was a ridiculous argument to make with a delusional man.

Castor gave a careless shrug. 'But he'll be alive and you can take comfort in having saved him. Now, I have other appointments to see to. If you will excuse me? Thank you for coming by. I look forward to seeing you and the Englishman tonight at the banquet where we will have one more opportunity to share a meal together. Think about my offer. Two days, Patra. Today and tomorrow. Remember, if I can't have you, no one will.'

She made it outside before her stomach gave out, retching up its contents with vehemence. She should not have come. She should not have tried to bargain with Castor. All it had proven was that he controlled everything about her life. Even when she fought him, he won, perhaps especially when she fought him. Nothing she'd done in the past twelve years had stopped his hold on her. The further she retreated from society, the more alone she was, the more victory he claimed. He wanted her to be alone, cut off from any support. He was a mad man. He would wait. Four years, five years, it wouldn't matter to him. He'd taken her husband, he had taken her baby. Now, he wanted to take Brennan. He preferred she be the one to make the 'choice'. He liked manoeuvring people into such corners where they chose their own unhappiness.

Two days! Two days to say goodbye, to convince Brennan to leave without letting on that this was Castor's bidding. If Brennan suspected that she'd gone to Castor, that this was part of a deal, he would be furious. He would go after Castor himself. Castor might even be angling for such a reaction. Then he'd be justified in 'defending' himself. This was all her fault, Patra thought, not for the first time. This was what she got for being happy, for letting down her guard just for a moment.

She couldn't let Brennan pay the ultimate price for her failure. But he would pay in other ways. It would destroy him to leave Kardamyli. He'd found a place for himself here and peace. Kardamyli made him happy. He would take her happiness with him, too, she realised. She wondered if she could be happy here without him. She certainly hadn't been before. She'd spent those years reclusively, trying hard not to call attention to herself. How could she go back to that now, knowing that it was what Castor wanted? That he was out there just waiting for her?

She stumbled away, hardly aware of where her feet took her. She had not realised how much Brennan had changed for her, how much of her happiness was tied up in *him*, in a person, not a place, not a cause. Love took too much out of one. It was the very thing she'd vowed not to allow and yet it had happened. She *loved* Brennan Carr. She'd said the words last night, but the understanding of what that meant had come upon her like the tide to the shore, not all at once, but in gradual waves until it covered the beach and there could be no retreat.

It was hard to catch her breath. She was climbing and crying, not an ideal combination for breathing. Her breaths came in gasps and sobs. What was she going to do? How could she get Brennan to leave without destroying him? It wasn't just leaving Kardamyli that would ruin him, it would be leaving her. She'd said she'd loved him and he'd been so desperate to hear it. To thrust him away now would obliterate the hope those words had brought to his eyes.

Patra stopped climbing and looked about her, trying to steady herself. She knew where she was. Brennan's hill, the place where Brennan liked to think. She'd not meant to come here, but her feet had picked this path anyway. And she wasn't alone.

Chapter Eighteen

Brennan stalked towards her, bristling with temper and relief, but it was his temper that got the better of him. 'Where the hell have you been? How do you think I felt waking up to find you gone with no note? No idea? I was worried sick.' For a man who was used to sleeping in two-hour naps, he was sleeping far too soundly these days if a woman could sneak out of bed on him.

'I went into town.'

'From the looks of you, that's not all.' He was regretting his outburst even if it had been provoked by concern. Patra looked terrible. Her face was pale, almost greenish, and she'd been crying. Then he knew what she had done and he felt almost as pale. 'You went to see *him.'* He jammed his hands into fists at his sides, impotent to reverse that choice. She didn't need to confirm his guess. The meeting had clearly devastated her. His gut clenched at the thought of her alone with the bastard, at the thought that he hadn't been there to defend her, to fight for her. But he was angry, too.

'You didn't trust me to handle it. What did you promise him to leave me alone? Because there's only one thing he wants and that's you.' Brennan threw back his head and gave a frustrated groan to the sky. 'Why couldn't you trust me to protect you? You say you love me, but what is that love worth? If you love me, let me defend myself, let me defend you.'

His words were harsh, painting her as a whore willing to bargain herself. 'Apollonius is *my* problem. I'm the one he wants to kill. I don't need you to beg for me.' Brennan paced the hilltop, pushing a hand through his hair. He was hurting her because *he* was hurting and now she was angry, too.

Tears came afresh and her voice trembled with emotion. 'I went to him and I denied I felt anything for you. When that didn't work, I begged him, because I love you! I ate a pastry for you, fed to me from his hand for the chance that you would be safe, and all the while he...' She couldn't get the rest out.

The words, the tears, broke his anger. This wasn't about him and his wounded masculine pride. This was about what Castor had done to her, what she had been willing to allow all for him. She had sacrificed for him and it humbled him to his core. He did not deserve her goodness, but he would fight to earn that right. Brennan shut his eyes, castigating himself. When he spoke, his voice was soft but forceful. He gathered her to him. 'Patra, I'm not a child.'

'I know.' Her voice was small against his chest. 'I don't want to lose you. You say I won't, but you don't know all that he is, all that he's capable of.' Her hand reached up to stroke his face, her eyes sad. He let her touch him, tolerated it for the moment. He was a boiling pot of emotions; other feelings competed with his anger. She had done what she thought was best out of loving concern for him at great risk to herself and she had paid for that risk.

He covered her hand with his where it lay against his face. 'Patra, let me be *your* man.' He broke from her long enough to retrieve his hidden blanket, long enough to force the anger out of his thoughts. She didn't need his rage. She needed a listener. He spread the blanket. 'Come and sit, Patra. Tell me everything that he is.' Perhaps in listening, he could figure out what to do. The only thing that was clear was that this was going to come to a head. He needed a plan, not just for himself, but for Patra.

She leaned against him, head resting on his shoulder, the truth she'd meant to tell him tumbling out. 'If I ate the pastry, he agreed to give you two days to leave. If not, he will come for you.' Her fist tightened in the folds of his shirt. 'He will come, Brennan. He will allow nothing to stand in his way.' She paused and he waited, sensing there was something more. He felt her body start to shake, sobs precluding the words that explained them.

'God, Patra, what else did he do?' Part of

him didn't want to know. That part wanted to run as far away from the evil as it could. But the other part, the part that wanted to be a man who stayed even through difficulty, understood that the tragedy had to be shared.

'There was a baby. When Dimitri left for Modon I was pregnant. I had just begun to suspect it. I only confided in Dimitri, partially in the hope that if it were true he would not go. But Dimitri told Castor.'

Cold horror uncoiled in Brennan's stomach as the realisation swept him. Castor had known Before Dimitri was killed. No, it wasn't possible. Brennan wasn't comfortable with the dark direction of his thoughts. How depraved did a man have to be to deliberately deprive an unborn child of his father? But Patra would not let him hide from them. 'I did not want to eat for days after Castor brought the news about Dimitri. But he begged me to eat. He tempted me with rich lamb stew and other foods. I relented for the sake of my baby. The baby was all that kept me going. I had to take care of Dimitri's child. One night not long after Castor had been bringing me food, I took ill. I thought it was the unfamiliarity of food in my stomach which had been empty for so long. But there was blood and it became something far worse. By the next day, the baby was gone.

'For a long time, I tried not to believe the worst. I told myself it was due to grief.' Patra shuddered, sobs racking her. Brennan held her close, letting his strength absorb her sorrow. 'Today, while he forced that pastry into my mouth, he told me what he'd done. He'd done it for us so there would be nothing between us, nothing of past reminders.'

He was going to kill Castor Apollonius. That was the plan. A man that depraved could not be allowed to live, could not be allowed to threaten others' lives. But he couldn't say that out loud right now, not to Patra, who had just learned of the new horror Apollonius had wrought in her life. No wonder she wanted him to leave. Apollonius was pure evil and pure evil could not be reasoned with. It could only be destroyed. Brennan kept his words calm. 'I am to simply go away and forget the life I made here, the love I made here, the love I *found* here? I am to leave you behind?'

'I bargained for your life. It was the best I could do,' she reminded him, her voice under control. 'It does not come without cost. Surely you would agree you are better off alive with your memories than dead at thirty.'

'I refuse to pay that price,' Brennan said softly.

'There is no choice. Castor won't fight fair. This won't be a duel with rules.' She lifted her head and fisted his shirt in her hands. 'Castor will come when you least expect it. He won't even come himself. He'll send some lackey who had been told he is ridding the world of an unpatriotic traitor. It could be anyone on the street. I won't ask you to live like that. The waiting, the wondering would drive a person mad long before a dagger did the job.' Patra shook her head. 'I'm not worth it, Brennan. I love you, but I don't want you to give your life for me. I want to know that you're safe. I want you to leave in the morning. Talk to no one. Just go, just disappear. I will make your excuses to Kon and Lydia.'

'Out of love for you, you want me to go?' His voice was dangerously quiet. 'But out of that same love, Patra, I choose to stay.' A plan was starting to percolate in his mind. The final choices were not clear to him, but the beginning point was. He needed to beard Castor in his den and the banquet tonight would be the perfect place to start.

If the stakes hadn't been so high or the company so repulsive, the banquet would have been a grand affair. Tables had been set up in the agora outside the tavern and the evening was fine. Lanterns were hung on ropes overhead to create light and candles lined the tables. Castor had spared no expense, Patra noted immediately. It made her nervous. 'He is trying to lobby the villagers with his largesse,' she explained in quiet tones to Brennan as they took their seats. 'He has an agenda.'

It was an old ploy of his to promote his influence. Money was good for anyone's economy. Fishermen might not like him, but Castor paid good money for the rare brown lobster he bought from them. Vintners might not approve of his politics, but they approved of his taste in wine and the price he'd pay not just for bottles of wine, but for casks of it. And his luxuries were for everyone tonight. All the villagers were offered a seat at the banquet. The villagers had shown up in their Sunday best, unwilling to turn down the elegant free meal and the chance to be part of what was sure to be prime gossip for the next several weeks. Patra wished the village had chosen not to show up. It would have been very gratifying to know the chairs went empty, the lobster uneaten. But to do so would have been outright rebellion against a powerful man and by extension a powerful organisation. She understood why they'd chosen to come.

She could barely eat. Castor had seated her and Brennan across from him in the centre of his table, his eyes on her constantly, making the rest of the table keenly aware of his interest. Beside her, Brennan, dressed in formal *foustanella* and embroidered shirt, fairly bristled with energy. She sensed he was planning something, although he'd said nothing about it to her.

That worried her even more. She didn't want rash actions. Nor could she forget that if Castor had his way, if she had *her* way to see Brennan safe, it would be her last night with Brennan. He had to be gone by tomorrow's end. She tried not to think that Brennan's leaving was something she and Castor had in common. He probably took perverse delight in having designed a goal they both shared.

Castor was determined to hold everyone captive as long as possible before delivering his news. Finally, as fruit and cheese were placed on the tables, Castor rose and called for attention. He was tall and commanding in the lights of the lanterns, his smooth orator's voice carrying easily across the agora to reach all the diners. He could be very compelling when he wanted to be, very believable.

'Several years ago we began the fight for independence. We won key victories and took our first steps. The men and the women of the Peloponnese stood up for what was right. They weren't afraid to die for it and they are heroes, every last one of them!' he began, to a round of applause.

Patra's eyes ran through the crowd. The

wine had been flowing freely. No wonder he'd waited until the end. He wanted people well lubricated.

'But the fight isn't finished. We aren't truly a free Greek nation yet. We have an Austrian king on our throne. We are governed by a monarchy.' He almost spat the word. 'A monarchy, by Zeus, to rule Greece, the birthplace of democracy! We have traded the Ottoman Empire for the Austro-Hungarian Empire,' Apollonius said emphatically.

He went on to enumerate the sins and failings of the monarchy, how it fell short of being a glorious beginning for independent Greece.

Apollonius ended, 'Nothing has changed except who we answer to. Greeks should govern Greece. It's time to take further action. But this time, I am not asking for an army.' There was more applause at that. Patra recognised the technique. He wasn't asking for the thing the people feared most—sending more men to die. Anything he asked for now would look small and reasonable by comparison. 'I have been charged by the head of our organisation with putting together a small force of men and going to Athens for the purpose of deposing King Otto. My organisation will be waiting to take over the government and structure it into a democratic body more in line with Greek ideals.'

Patra's hands clenched in her lap. Good lord, he meant to overthrow the king at best. At worst, he was talking about regicide. His blood thirst had no limits. Then his gaze fell on Brennan, dark eyes blazing with fervour for the cause, a passion rivalled only by his madness for her. 'I need men to come, Mr Carr. To have an Englishman with us would signal to Europe that we are ready to take the next step and govern ourselves without a king. You would not be the only private British citizen who feels this way. We have been aided by several in the past. This would be no different.'

He was calling Brennan out publicly. Patra's fists dug into the linen of the napkin in her lap. She shot Brennan a sideways glance to see if he understood the implications. 'What better way to prove yourself to the people of Kardamyli, Mr Carr? This is a chance to earn a place here, a chance to show everyone you are one of them.' He gestured to Brennan. 'You wear our clothing well enough. Are you more than just a man playing at village life?' It was a challenge thrown out to the villagers at large, but Patra saw its intent. It was designed to ostracise him, to make him an outcast. Brennan would be forced to go or forced to fight alongside Castor, a man capable of murdering his own soldiers. 'Unless, of course, you don't mean to stay?'

There were murmurs at that, undercurrents of people recalling the situation with Katerina Stefanos. Castor's eyes landed on her, a smile curving his lips, simulating fondness. 'Patra Tspiras is a woman worth staying for, you have my word on that. I fought with her husband at Modon. The cause has cost her much.' His voice took on a tone of privacy, making his next words sound personal, meant just for her, but voiced to the group. He put his hand over his heart. 'If I could bring Dimitri back for you, I would. I can't, but I can give you the Greece your husband fought and died for.' Such sentiment would go a long way with the crowd, many of whom had liked Dimitri or who had lost loved ones of their own.

His gaze flicked back to Brennan. 'Think about Patra and others in the village like her. What this could mean to her. She's already been through one war. She doesn't want to live through another. But she will, we all will, if the situation isn't resolved shortly.' He raised his arms and swept the guests with his eyes, his voice louder now. 'Good people of Kardamyli, tempers are boiling. Already in other places on the peninsula Greek factions are fighting each other over petty issues, provoked by a king who doesn't know how to rule.'

This was Castor's skill; making the extreme sound reasonable. He spoke the truth and used it for his own gain. It was hard to argue with his words. Patra knew he was right. Otto had been seventeen when he'd been offered the throne. His first years had been spent under a regency where others made decisions for him. That was five years ago. Otto was what? Twenty-two now? Twenty-three? He was younger than Brennan. He didn't have a clue how to live his own life, let alone govern a nation. Otto hadn't even been raised to be a king. He'd been in line for nothing until this came along.

Castor wasn't done. 'Each of you here tonight, think about what you can do to help your village take the next step towards being part of an independent nation. Give your loved ones and Greece the peace they crave. Give them a life where they won't be waiting for the next war. I will be here a few days more. Those of you—' his gaze fell back on Brennan '—who are interested in permanent independence should come to the tavern and see me.'

Beside her, Brennan stirred. He squeezed her hand once, pushed back his chair and rose. His voice filled the town square. 'Important decisions call for important thoughts. Before we leave tonight, I think it's important everyone have the facts. There are some glaring gaps in Captain Apollonius's reasoning and I think it's time you knew them.'

Patra swallowed hard in pride and in worry. She saw Brennan's intent immediately. He was going to turn the village against Castor. He was going to give them a reason to give in to their dislike of the man. Did he understand that even if his plan worked, he'd signed his death warrant? Castor would never let him live if he stole the village.

Across the table, Castor caught her eye, his eyebrow arched in intrigued query as if to say, 'This ought to be interesting, your lover fancies himself an orator. I will crush him anyway.' Every fibre of her being screamed that she should stop Brennan, beg him to sit down. But she could do nothing that wouldn't ruin him and make him appear weak. His reputation, his very life, was on the line now and she could only trust he knew what he was doing.

Chapter Nineteen

'Are you familiar with the dichotomy of false reasoning?' Brennan drawled with a smile. He had everyone's attention although Castor hadn't bothered to retake his seat. Perhaps Castor understood how much control he would yield if he did. Castor was a consummate showman. Still, Patra thought, Brennan came out very well in the comparison.

Anyone looking at the two men together would see the obvious differences. Castor was polished, every aspect of his appearance engineered for perfection, and yet, for all of Castor's perfection, for all of Castor's smooth talk and urbane manners, it was Brennan who exuded a sense of openness. When she looked at Brennan, with those stark, jutting cheekbones and those intense blue eyes, she saw an honest, open man. Would the village see that tonight? A cynic might suggest that openness came from his youth. He and Castor were on opposite ends in that regard. Brennan was just approaching his prime, perhaps still growing into it, whereas Castor was nearing forty and had all the confidence of a man who'd achieved his prime.

'Captain Apollonius would have you believe there are only two choices: march to Athens and demand the king step down, or remain here and tolerate incessant fighting as a few people scramble for crumbs from the king's table. I would suggest you examine the reasons the captain would have you embrace the choice to march,' Brennan said smoothly. 'He personally stands to gain much. The Filiki Eteria stands to regain their power, which has been minimised over the last few years. These are selfish reasons to depose a king. It won't change anything except who pulls the strings. The scramble for power won't stop, it will merely be different players. Nothing will change until the factions decide to work together. Until then, it doesn't matter who is in charge.

'You don't have to believe me. But ask yourselves, why would I say any of this? Why would I risk standing up against the captain? I have nothing to gain by disagreeing and everything to lose—your hospitality, your acceptance of me. If you want to take the chance that it will somehow be different with the Filiki in charge, go ahead and join Captain Apollonius.

'But before you do, you should know what sort of man he truly is. I think in your hearts you already do.' Brennan's gaze drifted from table to table, encompassing each of the guests in turn. 'I saw my friends slink out of the marketplace when he arrived, too afraid to meet his eyes, too afraid to be in his presence. That is not the usual reaction to a so-called war hero. Why are you afraid? Are you afraid he will spend other lives to achieve his own ambitions? He has done it before. He has bought your presence at this dinner with his wealth and promises of good food. What else will you allow him to buy out of your own sense of self-preservation? I say, do not give him an inch more until you truly understand what he is.'

The crowd was starting to shift. Patra could hear it in the rustle at the seats. Furtive glances were exchanged. She began to wonder, what other secrets did people hide in the village? How had Castor raised their fears? Was it possible he wielded power over others like he wielded it over her? Did others feel terrorised by him, as well?

'What is that I am? I am a politician, a warrior, a man with a cause just like the rest of you,' Apollonius called out. 'I have asked for volunteers, nothing more. No one is required to follow me. It is an honour I have asked you first.'

Patra made her decision. She would never know if others also suffered in silence. More than that, no one would ever know the full extent of Castor's evil if someone didn't break their silence first. She should not be afraid. These were her friends, her neighbours. Patra rose beside Brennan, reaching for his hand for support.

'Brennan is right. Your decision is yours alone, but Captain Apollonius is not the war hero he makes himself out to be.' She drew a deep breath, feeling Brennan's eyes on her, hot and intense, the grip of his hand firm and assuring. 'Twelve years ago, he deliberately put my husband on the front lines at Modon, knowing full well such an inexperienced soldier would be killed in the thick of the fighting. There are reports that prove this. What those reports don't tell anyone is why he did it.' She paused, gathering her courage. 'He did it so there would be no impediment to him pursuing me, although it was nothing I wanted or deliberately encouraged.' She could hear the low murmur of disbelief rumble through the crowd. 'It wasn't just Dimitri he put on the line that day at Modon, it was all the men of Kardamyli. The men who went with Castor, who fought with Dimitri, were sacrificed, too, for the sake of one man's coveting.' Her voice cracked at the last. 'I am so sorry. It was all my fault. It is *still* my fault that he comes here. I draw his attention to this village that would otherwise be left in peace.'

She sat down, unable to stand. Castor's voice filled the silence left in her wake. 'That's quite a story to tell, now after all this time when it serves her interest. She has a new lover and seeks to support him while blackening my own name.'

Brennan's hand moved to the dagger at his waist, but a voice in the crowd stalled the motion. Patra looked up to see Konstantine rise, his arms stretched out in a gesture for peace. 'Tempers are hot. We need to go home, each of us, and think about what we've heard. Maybe others have stories like Widow Tspiras.' He nodded towards her. 'You were brave to share your tale.' Then to the crowd he said, 'If you do, then you know she is speaking the truth. If you don't, then you may seek your truth somewhere else.'

Patra felt Brennan draw her to her feet, his arm tight around her. He was the first to set an example of leaving straight away and she was glad for it. She didn't want to face questions or stares from the villagers. She wanted to go home, wanted to be with Brennan.

They'd both taken a great risk tonight.

Lines had been irrevocably crossed. There were going to be consequences, but before she had to face those, she wanted pleasure one last time from the man who had stood up for her tonight and by doing so had given her the courage to stand up for herself publicly, directly. There would be no more passive resistance, no more subtle acts of defiance. It would be all-out war between her and Castor now. For the first time, the thought didn't fill her with fear.

Brennan bristled with energy beside her in the night. There was purpose in his stride, his hand tight around hers. Neither of them spoke on the short walk back to the house. Perhaps his mind, too, was reeling with the implications of what they'd just done. The evening was overwhelming enough without thinking of what came next. She wasn't ready yet to ask that question because she wasn't ready to hear the answer.

'You were magnificent tonight.' Brennan pulled her to him as they reached the house. 'I had hoped...' His words trailed off. He let his smile communicate his approval. 'It was a bold move, Patra.'

'No bolder than yours.' She twined her arms about his neck and drew him down for a kiss.

'Do you think it will be enough?' he asked between kisses, each one growing more heated than the last.

'I don't know, Castor is powerful. But you are, too, in a different way,' she murmured. 'Perhaps the people just need a catalyst to break through their fears.' The tip of his tongue traced her lips and she didn't want to think about Castor, about tomorrow. She only wanted to think about now.

Now was all he needed. There were plans that needed to be made and things that needed to be said, but this moment was for celebration, Patra's throaty laughter at his ear, her arms around his neck, his hands at her waist as he drew her against him for a long kiss. He'd wanted to give her freedom and he had. Better yet, she'd seized the opportunity tonight.

Something primal had welled up in him as he watched her at the banquet, so beautiful, so proud as she confessed Castor's treachery. Brennan covered her mouth in a bruising demand of a kiss, every fibre of his being concentrated on owning, on possessing, on leaving no question about his feelings for her. She was his and no plan they made, no consequence that followed, would change that.

'What are you doing?' Her words came in a breathy gasp, her breathing erratic in response to his rather physical overture.

Brennan breathed against her ear, his teeth catching its lobe with tiny, sharp nips. Rough play had its advantages, too. The premise was still the same: lovemaking had always been a good way to celebrate life's milestones. There was no reason to reinvent that particular wheel now when there was claiming to be done. He wanted to bind her to him, remind her tonight that they belonged together so that when the adrenaline of this victory wore off, she wouldn't retreat.

Patra leaned into him, her body fully against his, her mouth hungry. Brennan flicked his tongue in the shell of her ear. She moaned her assent, her encouragement. 'Ah, ah, Brennan, again, ah, yes, like *that*. Oh, sweet heavens, you are a genius with that tongue.'

Brennan laughed. He wrapped his hands beneath her buttocks and lifted her, feeling her legs instantly grip about his waist, both of them having reached the same conclusion: they weren't going to make it inside, let alone to a bed. Her skirts fell back and he pushed her up against the freshly whitewashed wall of the house. His mouth was at her neck, his hands working loose the neck of her blouse. She arched her neck, giving him full access, her gaze skyward, taking in the moon and the stars, and he took full advantage. This was decadence indeed to rouse a man to his fullest; a beautiful woman up against a wall, beneath the moon, the private places of her body bare against him, her breasts exposed to his ravenous mouth, her clothes nothing more than draping.

And she liked it.

More than liked it. She *delighted* in it. Her body, her cries, answering his heated rampage. He felt her hand move between them and his trousers came loose. He felt the warmth of her hand close around the length of his phallus, guiding him to her. He thrust, a piercing spear made all the sweeter for the roughness that replaced his usual finesse. She moved her hips with his, revelling in what this was: hard, honest sex and their bodies were starved for it.

One thrust, two, then three; he could feel his body tighten, climax would be swift and powerful. Her hands pushed back his unruly hair, anchoring in its thickness, but it was her eyes, flaming with life, her face full of awe, that held all of his attention as he drove into her. Every speck of his being—mind and body— was riveted on this moment, on the exertion of full-body sex. He held nothing back. The muscles in his arms bulged with the effort of their responsibility. Then he came into her a final time and her body crested with his. He let the force of her pleasure overpower him, drown him along with the power of his own enjoyment. The old forbidden hope began to fire deep in his soul, stoked to slow life by the woman in his arms. This time *would* be different. He would make it so. Some way, somehow.

Chapter Twenty

Even in his own exhaustion, Brennan still held her, his arms wrapped beneath her bottom, keeping her securely balanced between his body and the wall, his phallus still lodged within her, a wondrous feeling all its own to keep him there. She selfishly had no desire to move.

Patra moved her hands through Brennan's hair, smoothing it back from his face, loving the feel of its thickness beneath her fingers. Brennan could reduce everything to the most common of denominators. Nothing mattered but this, but him.

'Brennan,' she murmured against his ear. 'Why don't you take me to bed?'

Brennan's chuckle was warm and sensual. She felt his remarkable body stir. 'I was under the impression I already had.' But he complied anyway, carrying her inside, laying her down and 'taking her to bed' just as she requested. In fact he 'took her to bed' twice over, one of those times with his mouth.

She would be worthless by dawn. Under other circumstances, Patra would not have particularly cared except that goats didn't milk themselves and it seemed patently unfair that Brennan would sleep for twenty-minute intervals and wake up perfectly restored. He would look great in the morning, too, while she lay here wide awake, her mind going at full tilt. Dawn approached rapidly and sex could no longer hold reality at bay.

She had no illusions about what had prompted Brennan's rough, forthright possession tonight. He'd wanted to claim her, not just for himself and his own pride, but for her. He'd wanted *her* to know, wanted to mark her with his passion, and a most sensual brand it was, too. She was to be his and *only* his. He'd been a man in those moments of possessive sex and in the moments at the banquet when he'd fearlessly faced Castor Apollonius, not with a knife drawn in the heat of the moment, but with calculated rhetoric. His challenge had been premeditated, thought through. She had never loved him more than when he'd risen on her behalf and risked the truth. It took a far different sort of warrior to do what he'd done.

Patra traced the lines of his face with her finger, the long ridge of his nose, the rise of his cheekbones, marvelling when he didn't wake. She'd been wrong about him. In the beginning of their association, she'd thought him a boyish charmer. He was, but it wasn't the sum of him, not by half. Brennan Carr might smile, might flirt, might enjoy life to its fullest and have a penchant for spontaneity, but he was a *man* when it came right down to it. Not only because he could screw the hell out of her against a wall, on a beach or in a hammock, or in the ruins of a stone fort, but because he had an enormous capacity for love, for rightness and he'd chosen to bestow it on her. That choice had led them to this: a day of momentous decision. He stirred at last and groaned as if he, too, knew the question could not be avoided any longer: what did they do now?

'Brennan, we have to talk.' She settled her head in her favourite place against his shoulder. 'It's day two. After last night, Castor will be more determined than ever.' It was the thought they had not given voice to last night in the midst of their celebration, but it had to be said now before it was too late. 'You can be gone by breakfast.' It killed her to say the words, but he would not die for her. He was worth far too much to be wasted in a depraved man's vendetta.

Brennan reared up beside her, dislodging her from his shoulder. 'You want me to leave? After last night? After calling the village to acknowledge their fears and face them, you want me to do just the opposite?'

She sat up beside him. 'Your fears aren't here, Brennan.' It had occurred to her in the hours she'd lain awake in the dark that he was devoted to Kardamyli not only because he'd found a place here where he could be himself, but also because he'd found a place to hide. If he lost Kardamyli, he'd lose his protection. 'Your fears are in England, Brennan.' It was hard to say the words to him. She didn't *want* to send him away. Yes, she feared what would happen if he remained, if he didn't best Castor. But she also worried what would happen if he remained here, if he never went home.

'There are a lot of ways to lose someone, Brennan,' she said softly. 'If it isn't Castor, it's your past. If you don't face what has driven you away in the first place, you will never accept your own worth. I think you will regret your choice if you don't go home, Brennan.' Her words sounded suspiciously akin to something he'd told her once.

'I really don't think now is the time to talk about my personal issues. We have a mad man on the loose,' Brennan protested irritably. 'We need to spend our time talking about how to face him, how to face our future.'

Patra shook her head and held firm. 'Last night, you helped me take the last steps to becoming truly free. I want to return the favour.' She looked down at the sheet, pleating it between her fingers, her brow furrowing as she sought her words. 'When I first decided I could be with you, I promised myself I would let you go at the first sign of trouble. I've obviously broken that promise. Then, when I decided I could have you until Castor came back, I made another promise. I promised myself I would make sure you knew that you were worthy of love. I *will* keep that promise and I will not cheat you of it at the last, not when you're so close. If you don't go back to England and test the man you've become here with me, you will never truly believe you've achieved it.'

The silence stretched too long. Patra hazarded a look up. Brennan sat still. His voice was thick. 'When my friends married, I envied them. They'd found women who understood them at their core. I always wondered what it would be like to be with someone who understood me, insecurities and all.'

'How does it feel?' Patra ventured.

'Wonderful, awful,' Brennan confessed. She wanted him to *leave* her? He still couldn't get his head around the most important part of her message. Did she actually think there was even the slightest chance of that? What sort of man would that make him? Certainly not the sort of man he aspired to be and certainly not the sort of man he wanted her to think he was. Brennan cocked his head, his eyes steady on her. 'No. I will not run from this knowing that I leave you behind, still under Apollonius's power. More than that, I will not run from *us*. I will leave, but only if you come with me.' He could face England if she was with him.

He watched hope flicker in her eyes as she played with the idea of escaping. His hope rose, too. She hadn't said no. 'We could go to Siena, then on to Paris and England,' Brennan thought out loud, planning their route, plotting where they'd have support, where maybe he could work for money for the next leg of the journey. His funds would run low.

We. The little word was powerful and *empowering*. It was not a word they'd used between them. Always it had been him or her. He hadn't quite grasped the depth of his affections for her until he said that word out loud. He was willing to leave Kardamyli, his promised land, for her, to prove he was worthy of those affections. The reality of *we* was overwhelming for a man who had so recently eschewed commitment, but he embraced it, wanted to embrace it with her. 'We could do it, Patra. I can work along the way,' he assured her, but the hope in her eyes faltered.

'It wouldn't be enough,' Patra argued. 'As long as I'm alive, Castor will not stop.'

'As long as you're *here*, Castor won't stop,' Brennan amended. 'Castor is committed to his cause. He won't leave Greece, not even for you. It's all the more reason to leave with me. It's the only way.' At least it was the only way he could see at the moment and there wasn't a lot of time to plan. They would simply have to act. Unless, of course...

A dark thought crossed his mind and he had to give voice to it before the point of no return was reached; it was only fair to both of them, but it would only hurt one of them. Him. His old insecurities rose. He hadn't been enough.

'Do you *want* to leave with me, Patra?' Maybe all this talk of him leaving for his own good, his own development, had been a kind disguise for the truth. Maybe she loved him, but, like his father, didn't love him quite enough in the end. He understood that words often didn't measure up to the actions required of them. Weren't his father's haphazard promises proof enough of that? Understanding it didn't soften the blow. He almost drew away when she touched his arm.

'I think leaving with you is *impetuous*, Brennan.' It wasn't an outright rejection, but it was a warning that she was considering the costs of such rashness. She would be leaving behind her home, her entire adult life, even her country, everything she knew. In exchange, she would be thrust into a new world she'd never experienced, a new lifestyle. She would not have the comfort of a village around her, she would have only him. It was a daunting yet prideful realisation.

Brennan sought to give her courage. 'I am willing to give up Kardamyli for you, are you willing to give it up for me?'

She hesitated, her eyes filled with caution. 'That's not fair. Our decisions are not the same. You're leaving Kardamyli, but you have something to go back to. I'm not going back to anything. I am going forward, to nothing certain.'

Dear lord, he was losing her. A thousand thoughts filled his head; what did it say about her feelings for him if she preferred to stay and take her chances with Apollonius? Was there a way to stay and survive Apollonius? Something he'd overlooked? 'I'm not saying no, Brennan, but I need details. What happens to me if I walk out of here with you?' She looked down at her hand on his arm, a light blush creeping up her cheeks. 'In this part of the world, we have a saying that once you rescue someone, they're yours for life. Make sure you want the responsibility.'

'I do,' Brennan said swiftly, without hesitation. 'I want you, Patra. I will care for you, provide for you. I will be enough for both of us.'

'That's what you say now, maybe because it's a convenient argument. You are in the throes of your Greek honeymoon.' She stopped him with a finger to his lips, her eyes holding a warning. 'I do not doubt it, but I will not be your mistress, Brennan. I will not be a woman you visit occasionally and tote around as your living souvenir of the Grand Tour.'

'My mistress?' He was doing this all wrong if that was what she thought. He'd never meant to convey their relationship would be like that. 'I'm sorry I wasn't clear. That was not my intention.' He climbed out of bed, and knelt before her on one knee and naked. 'Will you be my wife, Patra? Marry me. Marry me before we leave. We can do it in secret if you have doubts.'

'Your proposal is as impetuous as you are,' she scolded but he could see the light return in her eyes, the twitch of her mouth as she tried not to smile.

'And it's as genuine,' Brennan prompted. 'I mean it, Patra. Marry me. Let me protect you with both my name and my body. Once the deed is done, it will be another barrier to Apollonius.' It wasn't a very good argument. Apollonius had already proved marriage didn't stop a sword. But he would say anything to persuade her and the clock was running. The sun was already up.

'A few weeks ago, you didn't want to marry. You were looking to escape it, in fact, rather desperately,' she challenged.

Brennan gave her a lazy grin. 'I hadn't met you yet.' He was slowly learning happiness wasn't a place, it was a person. He wanted her to learn that same lesson and he wanted that person to be him with every fibre of his being. Was this what it had felt like for Nolan when Gianna had been faced with the decision to leave Venice? For Archer and Haviland when they had chosen to stay in Europe instead of going home? He wished he could make the decision for her, but he didn't want her that way.

Brennan leaned in to press a kiss against the pulse at her throat. She was close to capitulating, to seeing the necessity of his plan. He wasn't above a reminder of the seductive variety to help that capitulation along. 'What is there to stay for, Patra?' he whispered.

Chapter Twenty-One

*N*othing that rivals the feel of your mouth on me. But that was no answer. One did not upend her life for a kiss, for sex. Those were not good reasons. A man might be able to do so. A woman had to be more practical. It seemed far too late for such considerations. Hadn't things progressed further than that even if the time had been short? It was hard to believe so much could change in such a little time, after years of nothing.

She'd always believed this affair would end with Brennan leaving, even before Castor had returned. She'd never envisioned it ending with *her* leaving. That was perhaps the real reason she stalled. She'd not lied. Leaving would be enormous for her. She'd never been anywhere outside the peninsula. However, if leaving was the only way to save him, perhaps then she could give herself permission to follow her heart. Saving him meant saving herself, too. He was offering her an escape. Brennan was right. What was here for her other than the known; the continued spectre of Castor Apollonius hovering over her life? What was there to stay for? She had no answer.

She reached for Brennan and drew him up from the floor, her arms going about his neck, drawing his head down so their foreheads met. She was going to do it. Her pulse raced with the knowledge of it. She was going to accept all he offered. 'All right, how do we do it?'

Brennan grinned his triumph. 'I have an idea. We'll need a ruse.'

Patra laughed in spite of the gravity of their situation. 'Another ruse? Because the last one turned out so well?' she teased. It had become quite complicated before it had become quite real.

'Precisely my point.' Brennan merely smiled and stole a peck of a kiss. 'I think it turned out splendidly, my dear soon-to-be Mrs

Brennan Carr.' She liked the sound of that. A new name for a new life. Patra Tspiras would remain behind in Kardamyli. But Patra Carr would see the world, as exciting and frightening as the prospect was. And Brennan Carr would have the chance to defeat his demons.

Brennan sobered. 'Now that the important things are settled, let's talk about the ruse. We'll have to leave separately. I'll depart first to satisfy Apollonius's timeline. I'll backtrack and we'll meet at St Spyridon. Here's how we'll do it...'

Castor Apollonius watched Konstantine Zabros's fishing boat sail out of the harbour in the late morning, a smug smile playing on his lips. Patra had done it. She'd got the intruding Englishman to leave, even after his rather impassioned speech at the banquet. Castor had been worried the man meant to stay. It wouldn't have changed the outcome. The Englishman would still end up dead, it would have just been more difficult.

He wondered if it galled her to know she'd helped him by getting her lover to leave. But

Patra had come through. She'd always been the self-sacrificing sort, always willing to put others' needs ahead of her own—Dimitri's, the cause, all of it had come before herself. She would sacrifice her own happiness to see the Englishman safe. Castor liked it when people acted as he predicted. And Patra had. In itself, it was an interesting testament to how much she cared for Carr. Castor had not doubted her for a moment. Patra would never willingly risk someone's life, even a stranger's.

Still, Castor felt the sting of it. The Englishman was no stranger and her choice was no random act of kindness. She *loved* Carr. He'd seen it in her face when she'd come to him, to persuade, to beg, to do whatever it took to save him. Then when she'd stood up last night and betrayed him with her accusations, and the Englishman had beamed at her as if she were an angel for trying to destroy him in front of the village. How that little outburst was going to play out remained to be seen. So far, there had been no volunteers for his journey to Athens, but the day was young and once the villagers realised Carr had told them not to run

away from their fears and then he'd done just
that, people would come around.

In the meanwhile, Patra's devotion to the
Englishman disgusted him. She'd never looked
at him the way she looked at Carr. She should
look that way for *him*, she should be willing to
beg for *him*, to eat phallic pastry for *him*. He
would do anything for her. He'd killed for her,
given her the freedom to choose him without
guilt—didn't that prove his devotion? And yet
she'd rejected him. Not only had she rejected
him, she'd replaced him with the upstart Englishman.

He'd retaliated by giving her a cruel di-
lemma: did she love the man enough to send
him away? Or would she let the Englishman
die for her? She'd chosen wisely. Carr wasn't
for her. What had she been thinking in the first
place? Carr was too young, too different. She
should be thanking him for making her do it
sooner rather than later. The Englishman was
bound to break her heart eventually.

The boat was a tiny speck on the horizon
and Castor's smile broadened. Brennan Carr
was on the boat. Patra had done a neat job of

it. They'd quarrelled in the agora, over what wasn't quite clear, but it had happened in front of witnesses and news had spread. They had parted ways, their flirtation short lived, hardly having survived the month. Castor had seen the smug, knowing smiles on the faces of the young girls who might have fancied Carr for themselves. He knew that particular attitude very well. If they couldn't have the handsome young Englishman, then they didn't want anyone else to either. They were glad the older widow had failed. The older women had closed ranks and consoled Patra. It all went the way these things go in small villages where everyone's lives are an open book.

That was the problem. Patra had done too neat a job of it. And so had Carr. He'd been suitably mad, swearing loudly he was done here, imploring Zabros to take him in the boat to who knew where, anywhere but here, apparently. He said all the things a man said when his heart was broken, or his marriage was tormenting him. Castor had heard enough men complain about women in his lifetime to know the script. Carr was executing it flawlessly.

Frankly, it made Castor suspicious. He knew why Patra had gone from lovesick sweetheart to disenchanted shrew in the matter of twenty-four hours. Patra was playing a part. But Carr? Carr, who had been on the verge of winning over the village? This about-face might have been executed with a perfection worthy of the stage, but that was just it. It was a performance only. How could it be otherwise? Castor knew from personal experience no one fell out of love with Patra that fast. If Patra was his, there was no way he'd leave her over one measly fight.

There it was in a nutshell: he wasn't entirely convinced Brennan Carr planned to be gone for good. What was that old folk wisdom about loving people? 'If you love them, set them free. If they're truly yours, they'll come back.' Fortunately, Castor had that contingency covered. That particular conclusion operated under certain assumptions. For instance, it assumed the newly freed *could* come back. It wasn't always possible. When it became clear Zabros was taking the boat, there'd been enough time for Castor to make some arrangements of his own.

Castor watched the boat disappear entirely from view. He took out his pocket watch. The possibility to return would diminish considerably in about two hours. Castor had a little something planned to ensure Carr's departure was of a more permanent nature than what he might have otherwise intended. Of course, Carr was welcome to come back; that was if he didn't drown first.

He shut the watch and put it back in his pocket. Patra would be devastated; a second man gone off to his death with her hot words in his ears. She'd not wanted Dimitri to go and she had made no secret of her displeasure. But Castor would be on hand to console her and this time, perhaps she'd come to appreciate what he had to offer her. He would forgive her words last night. Perhaps this time, she would know better than to refuse.

Castor let satisfaction fill him. He'd planned this brilliantly. He'd waited for her for twelve years. Just a few more minutes—and then she'd be his. His patience and ambitions were about to be rewarded. Patra would be his and with luck an outraged Britain would come to the Filiki's aid once it was learned an innocent Englishman abroad had been killed, perhaps by those who refused to heed the London protocols. The Filiki would have what they wanted and he would have what he wanted. He began the countdown in his head. Five, four, three, two, one…

Chapter Twenty-Two

The explosion caught Patra unawares in the marketplace, the sound of it tearing through the agora even from a distance. For a moment she was struck dumb with ignorance. What could that be? She'd been lost in her own thoughts. Her own drama had made the world recede. Then people around her began to scream. Above the din of sudden panic, she heard the words, 'The harbour!' Her next thought was Brennan. That was when she began to run.

Running seemed to make her brain work better, too. Everyone was running, the street down to the harbour was crowded. Later, she would think how it made little sense to run towards trouble. People ought to have been running away from it. But at the time, they had no idea what it was. She wished it could have stayed that way.

Patra pushed her way through the crowd out on to the pier. 'What has happened?' She found a man with a spyglass and tugged at his arm until he answered. Her voice rose in panic as her eyes caught sight of the smoke plume rising up over the water. How could something go wrong? He'd only just left. Konstantine and he had sailed away not even twenty minutes ago. The boat was still visible from shore. The boat... Her stomach tightened with sickening realisation.

The man beside her lowered the spyglass and gave a slow, shocked shake of his head, his words confirming her fear. 'Zabros's boat has exploded.'

The plume of smoke took on new meaning for her. The boat was destroyed, blown to bits. 'Survivors?' she asked desperately. But she already knew. How could there be? She'd heard the force of that explosion all the way in the market. She didn't wait for an answer. She snatched the spyglass from his hand and held it to her eye. She wished she hadn't, but Patra forced herself to look anyway; forced herself to look at the splintered planks of wood, at the sailcloth limp and heavy in the water; forced herself to search the water for the only thing that mattered—a body, proof.

She swung the spyglass wildly over the waters, seeking horrible confirmation, or horrible hope that, somehow, Brennan had managed to escape. She needed to see him, needed to know. She'd not seen Dimitri again even in death. He'd been buried at Modon. The helplessness she'd felt when she'd learned of his death crept over her, determined to claim her. He'd been dead weeks before she'd known it. But not this time. Brennan's death would not go unmarked as his had. She would bear witness to it.

The first piece of proof lay near the sails. A shirt, white like the sails. Perhaps it was only sails. She let the spyglass linger on it until she was disappointingly sure. It was indeed a shirt and Brennan was always so fond of not wearing his. Of course it would have been off. An image of him in those last unsuspecting moments filled her mind: Brennan shirtless, his auburn hair messy from the breeze, his muscles flexing as he hoisted a sail, the sun on his skin, his laughter on the wind. He would be laughing, somehow she just knew he would have been. And maybe he'd been thinking of her, thinking of them being together again. *'In two short days, we'll be together always.'* Those had been his last words. They weren't supposed to be his last words to her for ever. He was supposed to double back and meet her at St Spyridon's. He would, he promised, she told herself fiercely.

It was only a shirt, some part of her tried to argue. Shirts weren't bodies. Hope was indeed a resilient thing. Her fingers had the spyglass in a death grip. The man beside her attempted to pry it from her, but she wouldn't let go. Brennan had to be out there somewhere, she would not let go until she found him. Panic, grief, guilt made her wild and strong. By God, she'd swim out there and drag his body back herself if she had to. It was the least she could do, to atone for her failings both past and present. She should never have let Brennan put himself in the middle of this. She should have turned him away from the beginning. The old guilt, the old arguments swamped her and she started to tremble. She'd *known* how this would end, she could have stopped it by not starting it.

Her jerky sweeping motions slowed. *She* could have stopped a boat from exploding? Did she truly believe that? Her hand stilled on the spyglass as she realised what that thought meant, what conclusions it led to. If she could stop it, it meant she had caused it, had somehow been responsible for it. There was only one way she could have caused such a thing to happen. Castor had done this.

A new type of grief overtook her. This wasn't about an accident claiming Brennan and Kon. This was about one man's diabolical, covetous revenge. The thought made her sick. She felt her stomach roil and clench, then she was on her knees, retching on the wharf, the spyglass rolling out of her grip. She didn't need it any more. She *knew*. While everyone around her speculated their fears about what had happened, she knew. Oh, God, she knew.

She went to pieces then: retching, sobbing, gasping her grief and her anger in incoherent sounds. Somewhere in her mind, there was an errant thought that she should go to Lydia. Konstantine had been on that boat, too. But she couldn't get to her feet. She was incapable of anything but making terrible sounds.

A cry went up near her and she rallied the last of her sanity. The man with the spyglass knelt beside her, gentle hands at her back. 'There's a body floating in the water. I'm sorry.'

Patra yanked on his lapels, holding him close in her wild misery. 'Only one? Not two?' Brennan was a good swimmer. But the next moment she hated her thoughts. What kind of a friend was she to hope that body was Kon's and not Brennan's?

'No one survives an explosion like that.' He was trying to loosen her fingers, but she held on. Someone was screaming. Was that her? Hands closed about her, arms pulled her away, strong arms, a man's arms.

'Patra, it's awful, I came as soon as I could. Come with me, let me take you somewhere quiet.' She should not trust those tones meant to soothe and cajole her into peace. She should fight, but her strength was gone.

Castor knelt beside her, his face close to hers. She did fight then, the sight of him summoning her anger, giving it power over her grief. 'You did this!' She struck out at him with a fist, catching him across the jaw. He fell backwards from his crouch. Her mind was too full of thoughts to pick one; she had to get away. She had to make Castor pay. She had to find Brennan. In her anger, she flung herself at Castor, fists pounding, nails scratching. She cursed him with every suitable word she knew. 'You killed him, you killed him! You whoreson! Murderer!'

In her anger and her fear, she was no match for him with his cool logic and playacting. 'Patra, you don't know what you're saying.' He let her pound him once more with her fists before catching her wrists in his grip. 'You're in shock.'

'You killed him!' She struggled to get free and couldn't. He was too strong and she was too spent. Would no one help her? Couldn't anyone see he was murderer twice over?

'Patra, let me help you,' he coaxed. But she would not be helped. He wanted to lead her away from the crowd, but she couldn't allow that. Brennan would never find her if she did that. Patra dug in her heels, refusing to budge. 'I can't leave. He might be out there, Brennan might be out there.' Her voice broke.

Castor's voice was low at her ear, her body crushed to his in an attempt to restrain her. 'He *is* out there, Patra. I assure you. But he is not alive. Let someone else find him.'

She felt the strength of his grip on her shoulder where shoulder meets neck. It was too tight, too painful. She was starting to see black in her vision. 'You killed him,' she managed to say once more before her body became impossibly heavy and everything went dark. But it didn't matter. Nothing mattered any more. Everything that mattered had been on that boat. It was over.

It wasn't over. Patra was somewhat surprised by the realisation, her mind waking up before she risked opening her eyes. What wasn't over? Now her mind was waking up too fast. She would have preferred the blissful fog of half-sleep. Now it came back to her. Brennan was dead. Was that true? There was no body. Correction, there was one body. There was a shirt, *his* shirt. Where there was one body, there was bound to be another. She'd seen the debris. If she could have looked longer, if she'd had more time, she would have found him. She knew it. Perhaps she should be glad she hadn't found him, hadn't seen the physical perfection of him ruined, his body torn apart.

Her stomach started to churn again, nauseated at the thought of Brennan destroyed. She fought back the urge to vomit. It would require movement, sitting up, rolling to her side. Too much effort. She didn't want to make any effort ever again for anything…

Brennan threw the tavern door open, bellowing and wet, followed by a dripping Konstantine.

'Where's Patra?'

He strode through the taproom, underestimating the effect the appearance of a dead man can have on a crowd, let alone two. The room fell silent. He hadn't the patience for it. The moment he and Konstantine had made the shore, he'd run to the house only to find it empty. He'd even chanced a visit to the hill, but there'd been no sign of her. Fears had started to ignite. The tavern was his last hope.

'Apollonius!' Brennan yelled, his foot smashing open the parlour door, his knife drawn. He wanted to find her here and Apollonius with her. He wanted to end it. But the parlour was deserted. There was no sign she'd ever been there. Brennan lowered his knife and faced the taproom. 'Where is he? Where is the murdering bastard?'

'He's gone,' a man called out. 'Our guess is that he left while we were still preoccupied with the boat explosion.' And Brennan's guess was that Patra was with him.

'How is it you're still alive?' another called out. Brennan left the explanations to Konstantine, how a last-minute shipment of barrels needing transport had been rolled aboard. But

Brennan and Kon had been on the alert for some trickery and it hadn't taken them long to row out far enough to vacate the boat without being noticed. They'd evacuated just in time and watched Kon's boat explode at a safe distance.

'But what about the body in the water? We saw it,' another put in.

'His secretary,' Kon supplied grimly. 'The body was already dead and stuffed in one of the barrels.' That had nearly made Brennan retch.

'And now he has Patra,' Brennan put in, bringing everyone's attention back to what mattered most. There could be no doubt now that Patra had told the truth last night. She was gone and the bastard hadn't even blinked about murdering his secretary just to have a body floating in the water to convince everyone Kon and Brennan were dead on the off-chance they weren't. The more Brennan thought about it, the more he believed the body had been put there for Patra's sake—to persuade her instantly there was no hope of survivors. Such proof would break her.

Brennan shoved his knife into its sheath. She must be terrified and she would be destroyed with guilt. She'd been in the marketplace, she would have seen the explosion, even the body at a distance. She would think he was dead, that there was nothing to fight for. She would blame herself. It was a nightmare come to life for her again. 'I am going after her. When I find her, I am going to kill Apollonius.' Never mind, he didn't know where to look. He hadn't the faintest idea of the direction Castor had headed.

A man rose from a table—Alexei Katsaro. 'He would have headed overland. The harbour was too crowded, too busy. He would have been noticed trying to put out in the boat.'

Brennan nodded and turned to go. 'Thank you.'

'Wait,' Alexei called out. 'I'll go with you. You said some things last night that have needed saying for a long time. We won't be pawns any more.'

'I'll go, too.' Spiro Anastas stood. 'You've taken care of my old mother when we've sent her to the market with few coins. This is the least I can do for a friend.'

Another man rose. 'You fed my children when my wife was sick and I was gone for months for work.'

'You helped me with my olive harvest when my son was hurt.'

'You gave my son a job mending nets.'

'You played with my children.'

Men rose, voices filled the tavern; their kindness overwhelmed Brennan. 'Those were simple acts,' he protested. He didn't warrant praise for them. Old women didn't deserve to starve, boys needed their pride as they became men. He'd only done what was right.

'They still needed doing and you did them,' Spiro Anastas said solemnly. 'We're coming with you. We've all lost so much to Captain Apollonius, we aren't going to lose you, too.'

The innkeeper brought him a leather bag and a canteen. The barmaids were already distributing canteens to the others. Kon slapped him on the back with a grin. 'Haven't you learned you can't do anything in this village alone?' Then he sobered. 'You're one of us,

Brennan. You don't need to marry for it, you don't need to take up a cause for it. You've already proven it just by being you.'

'We have to find her, Kon,' Brennan murmured, slinging the leather satchel over his shoulder bandolier-style.

Kon put an arm around him. '*We* will.'

Chapter Twenty-Three

She was waking up, remembering the rest of it: why she hadn't had more time to find Brennan. *Castor*. He'd been there, dragging her to her feet, resisting her meagre attempts at annihilation, imprisoning her in his arms. The world had gone black.

She didn't have a choice. She had to open her eyes. Had to figure out where Castor had taken her. She was surprised to note that apparently something did still matter. A little flame of life still flickered inside her. She had to avenge Brennan. She had to stop Castor from killing innocents again.

Patra pushed herself up, eyes opening, her body physically aware of her surroundings for the first time. This was no bed she was on, but a stone slab, a ledge cut from the side of a wall. It was dark except for the light of a lantern. A cave, perhaps? She swung her feet over the edge of her makeshift bed and found floor. It wasn't a high ledge, then. There was something liberating in the knowledge. She was free to move around. The ledge wasn't meant to be her prison.

It was a silly reassurance. What did that mean? What could she do with her freedom? She was in a cave with no idea of her location. How far from Kardamyli had Castor brought her? Were they close to the sea? Up in the hills?

A shadow merged into her vision and took form. Of course she wasn't alone. Castor stood there just beyond the candlelight, arms folded, watching her with those dark eyes. 'You're awake. I was beginning to think you weren't going to wake up.' He gestured to the table. 'Come, eat. You need your strength.'

Eat? It seemed like a herculean feat at the moment. No matter how alive her mind was, her body was weak. Simply sitting here had taken extraordinary effort. 'I'm not hungry, I don't think my stomach could take anything.'

'Patra, you must try.' His voice was silky, full of concern, as he pleaded with her. She thought she saw the whisper of a patient smile on his cruel mouth. 'You and I have been down this path before. And I'm sorry for it. I would not wish such sadness on you, certainly not twice. But I will help you through, just as I did before. I will be here for you in your grief. You know you have to eat. You don't want to become ill like you did the last time.'

He picked up the tin plate and advanced towards her, holding it out like a peace offering. It might have been the most terrifying thing he'd ever done in front of her. Involuntarily, she shuffled away until her back was pressed against the stone wall of the cave. How did he have the utter gall to act as her friend, her caregiver, when he had murdered the two men she'd loved?

He sat beside her and she had no place to go. Her skin started to crawl. How had she ever thought him handsome? Gallant? He was none of those things. He was a man corrupted by power, a man who would use that power to get the one thing he didn't have.

He speared a piece of meat with a fork and held it out to her. 'At least this time, you aren't breeding.' He paused. 'You're not, are you?'

'No. Of course not. We were careful,' Patra said with wary conviction. This had happened before, this offering of food, this concern over her fertility with another man. But this time, she knew the depths of Castor's evil. Under no circumstances would she, could she, eat any food he offered her. She brought her hand up under the plate with a forceful slap that sent its contents into his face. She dashed off the ledge, acutely aware that she moved too slowly. She couldn't dash at all.

Castor was too fast. He was on her, taking her to the ground with a rough thud. She broke her fall with her hands and knees. Castor had her about the waist, on her like a dog. She wished she could see him. If they were face to face, she could slap him, spit at him. 'You bastard!' Patra shrieked and struggled, but she couldn't dislodge the iron grip of him about her waist, the strong press of his body. She could feel his arousal against her buttocks.

The man was vile. How could he even think she'd consent to anything with him after what he'd done? 'We will never come together. I will never be yours!' But he was so heavy against her. She swallowed her fear, it was threatening to overtake her anger. What could she do? She was starting to feel helpless. Struggles only weakened her, yet not to struggle would be worse. He would make her pay most intimately this time for provoking her. His free hand moved between his thighs and her bottom. Trousers worked loose.

'I don't think there's anything you can do about it.' His mouth was at her ear, his body entirely over her now, his hand beneath her skirt, pushing it up.

Could she beg? She would, anything to stop this. He'd already taken Brennan from her, her pride was expendable at this point. 'Please, Castor. Don't do this. You don't want me like this…like a dog in an alley.' She choked the words out. Her throat started to close with tears.

She didn't want to remember sex this way, disgraced and shamed. This was not intimacy. To Castor this was about power and domination, proof he could force even her to his will. She wanted to remember it the way it had been with Brennan, laughter and heat as they struggled together for that final release.

'I must have you immediately,' he grunted at her ear. 'You can never really be sure, Patra, if the Englishman's seed has survived. We can at least muddy the waters a bit should you be wrong.' His hand slipped between her legs, wet and sticky where it touched her. 'We'll help you along, my dear. In time, you won't need it. You'll rouse to me on your own.'

'No, no, please, no.' It was a pitiful, mewling litany of a protest. She hadn't the strength left for more. All she could do was scream. If she was lucky, he would be mercifully fast. It would be over quickly and she could get to the business of trying to forget. Whatever he did to her only had the power she gave it. She closed her eyes, her arms tensing. Nothing came but words from a voice she thought she'd never hear again.

'Get your unholy body off of her.'

Patra's eyes flew open, her physical sense more sure than her brain's rationale of what it registered. As illogical as it seemed, Brennan was here and he had a gun. No, wait. He had two.

He was going to kill the rutting bastard. Brennan advanced on the lurid scene in front of him with a cold clarity he'd only felt a few times in his life, such as the time he'd leapt the horse off the Dover dock. Failure was not an option. But unlike that leap in Dover, he had a plan this time and he knew what he was doing. He also had reinforcements. Half the village waited outside the cave, armed and ready to deliver justice if he could not. But Castor was his first. He'd had a day and a half of hard tracking to think it through, to imagine this moment, to walk himself through every aspect of it, to steel himself against the horror of it. And yet, despite his mental preparations, the reality exceeded the horror.

To hear her screams as he approached the cave had been bone chilling. Was he too late? He'd regretted every rest he and the men had taken, every moment they hadn't been moving towards her. He'd told himself he was here now, that was all that mattered. To see Castor on her like a dog, to see her sobbing and without choice, had nearly destroyed him. He held on to cool detachment by the slimmest of threads.

He was gambling on the element of surprise with his first shot, not a mortal wound. A fatal shot would not be possible yet, not with Patra so close to Apollonius. 'Patra! Get ready to move!' he barked, giving neither of them time to think before he fired the first pistol, and kept moving forward, tossing the empty weapon aside as he came.

The bullet passed close to Apollonius's shoulder. He jerked backwards as the bullet breezed past, a natural reflex in even the most battle hardened of men. His defensive reflex provided an opening for Patra. She struggled out of his loosened grip, rolling away. Apollonius reached for her, but Brennan was faster, pushing his body between them. 'Stay behind me, Patra!' This was going to be over fast. It wouldn't even be a fight. It was not intended to be. It was intended to be revenge.

'*You* are supposed to be dead.' Apollonius staggered to his feet, his immaculate clothing askew, his dark hair in his face. For the first time, his appearance matched the part, his derangement obvious. The mad man was exposed.

'You broke your word.' Brennan kept the pistol on Apollonius. He had Patra and the exit behind him, and beyond that another surprise. The men of Kardamyli waited to bring Apollonius down if he didn't make it out, but Patra would make it. She would be safe. He could ensure it with his own life if necessary. Brennan took a step backwards, feeling Patra move with him. How far did they have to go? Ten steps before they could turn and run? 'You promised the lady you'd let me live if she made me leave.'

'Well, she didn't make you leave. You are, regretfully, still here.' Apollonius gave a dry laugh, his eyes slanting towards the gun. 'I don't think you'll do it, by the way.' Then his mouth turned up in a hard smile. 'You'll have to, though, you know that, don't you? You can't possibly think to outrun me or the brotherhood on the road. I will hunt you down, Englishman.' He flicked his eyes towards Patra. 'Do you love her enough to kill for her? I do.'

'You're a sick man, Apollonius.' Brennan swallowed hard and took another step backwards. He had been thinking just that, adjusting his plan now that he had Patra behind him. Maybe they could run.

'I am the liberator of the peninsula. I drove the Turks from our land. I'm a hero in these parts.' Apollonius was starting to move now, to step closer for every step he took backwards. Brennan's hand clenched around the pistol. Patra was four or five steps behind him, closer to the exit, safer. His mind reached for cool detachment. He didn't want to think about what he was doing. Thinking had never been much help.

'Did you ever think you'd got this wrong? That this isn't about you or me having her? What did you call it last night? The fallacy of dichotomous reasoning? The idea that we convince ourselves there's only two options.

One or the other. You think it's about me killing you or you killing me. You're thinking only one of us walks out of here.' Evil fire lit in Apollonius's eyes. He made a lightning-quick move, something silver flashing in his hand, a blade. 'There's a third option, Carr. No one has *her*.'

Brennan didn't think. He just fired, the bullet taking Apollonius in the chest. The man was dead before he hit the ground, but the blade had left his hand a moment before the bullet hit its target and had taken on a life of its own. It flew towards Brennan's shoulder, its trajectory too high to hit him, but not too high to hit Patra at a distance behind him. *God. No.*

He had to stop that knife! He had no weapon, no shield, only his body. He threw up his arm, his hand closing around the hilt of the knife in a miraculous, perfectly timed grab. He would never be able to duplicate that grab again in his entire life. He hoped he'd never have need to.

'Brennan!' Patra staggered towards him, reaching for the hand that held the knife, eyes searching for blood. Her hands were all over him, looking for injury. 'Are you all right?'

He gathered her to him, fearing she'd fall. 'I'm alive.'

'You're not supposed to be.' Her voice was a whisper of disbelief as he guided her out of the cave. He didn't want to stay there a moment longer, didn't want to subject her to its foul reminders.

'I am here and I've brought reinforcements.' He was glad for those reinforcements when they reached the outside, glad for Kon's strong arm about him, glad for the canteen of water someone held out to Patra. He was starting to shake, his body going crazy with adrenaline.

The air was cooler out here, the stars were bright. The moon had risen. The night centered him. He found a group of rocks where he and Patra could sit privately away from the men, where he could hold her and they could let the shock and the joy take them. There was so much to absorb if they let their minds open to the events of the last two days. It was hard to take in, but he had to try because it could not be ignored. He couldn't pretend a man hadn't tried to kill him, hadn't tried to rape his wife—his almost-wife by legal standards, though in his heart the marriage was already done—that he'd had to take a life to protect her.

Patra laced her fingers through his. 'What were you thinking, to catch that knife? You could have lost a hand, a finger.' She was trembling beneath the blanket draped over her shoulders.

'I was thinking I could have lost you.' Brennan smoothed her hair back from her face. 'That would have been far worse than a finger. I'd still have had nine others. And I'd still have had one hand if it had come to that. But there is no other you, Patra. I could have lost *you*.' The enormity of what Apollonius had put them through was starting to creep up on him. It was harder to hold the events at bay when they came attached with emotion.

'I did lose you.' Patra's eyes began to brim with tears. She covered her mouth with a shaking hand. 'Oh, God, Brennan, I don't think I would have survived it.' Her eyes widened, reliving the horror of those early moments.

'Don't think about it, Patra. You didn't lose me.' Brennan squeezed the hand that held his. 'I'm here.'

'But you shouldn't be. I don't understand. I saw the boat.' She took a gasping breath. 'Kon! He was on the boat, too. Is he...?' Her voice trailed off, unable to make the word.

'He's fine.' Brennan held her gaze, letting his own gaze steady her. 'We were not on the boat, Patra.'

'There was a body. I saw it in the spyglass,' she argued.

'It was in one of the barrels that were loaded on the boat and when the boat exploded, it did, too. As you know, Konstantine was supposed to make a cargo run.' It had been part of their plan, that after the quarrel he would go out with Konstantine on the cargo delivery. He just wouldn't come back. 'Well, that morning Apollonius had some items he needed taken to one of our stops. He brought them down while we were loading. Rather, his men did. I was immediately suspicious. When I told Kon, he was willing to test my hypothesis.'

'But I saw you leave, I saw the two of you sail away.'

'When we were far enough out, we lowered the rowboat over the far side and rowed away. We watched from a distance. If the boat was harmless, we'd row back and complete the deliveries. I'd go on to meet you in secret as planned. If it wasn't, then we'd have our proof Apollonius was indeed a villain.'

'You took a huge chance. What if the boat had blown up before you were safely away?'

'Don't worry over it, it didn't happen.'

'But for a while it did. It happened to me. I lost you,' Patra said fiercely.

Brennan nodded. 'I know.' He understood what she was feeling. For a while, he'd lost her, too. 'I came back as quickly as I could. Kon and I reached the village by afternoon, determined to string Apollonius up. But he was already gone and you with him.' Brennan shook his head. 'I can't put into words how I felt in those moments. I'd been so sure Apollonius's influence in our lives, in your life, was nearly over after we'd made our plan, only to learn that it was not. In fact, it was more powerful than ever. He had you. The man you hated the most *had you*.' The woman he loved was in the clutches of the man she'd fought, resisted, for years. If he had ever doubted his affections, that realisation had cleared them right up.

His confession touched her. Her fingertips stroked his face. 'But you came for me.' Her voice was soft, her steady strength returning to her because she thought he needed her strength, his beautiful, selfless Patra, lending her strength to others. To him. 'We are fine. We are both fine and Castor can't haunt us any more.' Something powerful flickered in her eyes. 'I am free.' She smiled and raised her head to the night sky, exulting in the realisation, and Brennan celebrated, too. She wasn't the only one who was free. Because of her. He was free from the past. He was free now to be the man he wanted to be, her man, a man with purpose and direction because he was with her.

'Where do we go from here?' he asked. He nodded towards the men milling about their campsite. It occurred to him that if Castor was dead, she needn't refashion a brand-new life away from all she knew. 'We can go back to Kardamyli.'

'I think England is still our destination,' Patra said softly. 'Castor has connections.'

'We could stay. I think the village would protect us if anyone came looking.' Brennan was almost certain of it.

'Not yet,' Patra conceded. 'We need to let things die down here and *you* need to go to England. We've already discussed this.' He knew in his heart that Patra was right. It would be best if he disappeared for a while. England would be far safer. But there was reassurance, too. He would be back. *They* would be back and, in time, they would make the life here that he dreamed of.

'England it is.' Brennan smiled. He was going home. For the first time in two years, the thought did not fill him with dread. He understood his father better now even if he couldn't condone his father's choices. The love of a good woman was a powerful love indeed. He hoped when the time came, he'd be a better father because of it.

Patra placed a soft kiss on his mouth. 'England tomorrow, but tonight, I need you to do something for me.'

'Anything,' he breathed against her lips. The campsite was far away.

'Make love to me under the stars.'

'Are you sure?' His body was primed and bursting with the need to release the adrenaline of the fight, but he'd suspected after Castor's treatment of her, she would not welcome it. Maybe not for a while.

'There are things I need to tell you about Castor, about Dimitri, later, some day. But tonight, I need you, just you.' It was all she had to say. He knew the rest. She needed him tonight to be the lover that erased the fear and horror of Castor's assault. It had been an incomplete action, but that didn't make it any less horrifying.

'I thought you'd never ask.' He grinned against her mouth, their foreheads pressing together. Tonight he would be that man for her and every night hereafter.

Brennan retrieved a blanket and shook it out. Patra laughed, a throaty sound that warmed the night. Two days had been too long without it. 'Do you go everywhere with a blanket?'

'It always seems to come in handy.' Brennan held out his hand. 'Come join me.'

'Not yet.' Patra loosened the string on her blouse, flirting boldly with him. She pulled the blouse over her head, her breasts dusky in the moonlight. Brennan's breath hitched as he watched her undress, slowly, deliberately, for him alone. 'I have it on good authority it's easier naked.'

He put his hand on the buckle of his belt and the *foustanella* dropped. 'Show me,' Brennan murmured.She moved into him then, kissing him hard on the mouth, her hands anchoring in his hair and, to his everlasting pleasure, she did. Tonight had been his last escape. God willing, he'd never need an escape plan again.

Three days later, he made certain of it. Brennan Carr married Patra Tspiras on the beach in Kardamyli, surrounded by the village, dressed in a *foustanella*, his bare feet sinking into the sand. Beside him, her hand in his, Patra wore an overdress with an embroidered bodice and a white shift beneath, her hair loose beneath a linen veil. She looked stunning, she looked *happy*, like a bride should, like *his* bride should. He'd never dared to dream he might be such a lucky man, that someone might love him so thoroughly.

The marriage was unorthodox by the priest's standards. He would have preferred they be married *inside* the church, and he would have preferred Brennan be Greek, but Brennan had been persuasive and compromises had been reached. Brennan was Greek enough for the village and that was all that mattered. The priest placed the *stefana*—the crowns—on their heads and said the prayers that made them man and wife as tiny warm waves rippled over their feet. Brennan closed his eyes, his hand tight over Patra's, wanting to capture this moment in its entirety, the moment his heart knew he was home.

There was partying in the agora afterwards, joyous hours filled with ale and wine, cakes and dancing before the town escorted them to their wedding night on 'Brennan's Hill' beneath the stars.

'Alone at last.' Brennan smiled at his bride as the voices of the singing townsfolk faded off into the night.

'Never alone,' Patra said softly. 'Not as long as I'm with you.' Her hands untied the laces of her bodice and she slipped out of the overdress, her shift flowing loosely about her, made transparent by the moonlight.

Brennan swallowed hard against his rising desire. He had all night. 'I have a gift for you.' He bent beneath his bush and pulled out the blanket and a large basket.

'The hill gets better and better provisioned,' Patra teased as Brennan went through the market basket.

He handed her a carefully wrapped package. 'I brought it from Venice.' Venice seemed a lifetime ago. 'At the time I didn't know why I bought it. I saw it in a window and it compelled me. I saved it, hoping there would be cause to give it to someone.' Hoping, but never actually believing he'd find a woman special enough to wear it.

Patra smiled at him and undid the string. The wrapping fell away and she sighed. 'Oh!

It's beautiful.' She held the white-silk night-gown against her. 'I shall save it for England. Thank you, Brennan.'

'There's a story behind it...' Brennan began, thinking of what happened to the first night-gown he'd bought. This one was the second.

Patra pressed a finger to his lips. 'Save it for later. I have a gift for you, too.' She went to a bush of her own and pulled out a much smaller basket. She took out a jar of thyme honey. 'You'll have to lie down for it, though.' Her eyes sparked wickedly.

'I have to lie down for honey?' Brennan teased, an idea starting to take shape in his mind as he stretched out on the blanket. 'There's nothing to put it on.'

She gave him a hot look that had him in-stantaneously hard. 'There's you.' She dipped a finger in the jar. It came up gold and glis-tening. She put the finger in her mouth and sucked. His pulse skipped. Sweet heaven, he was going to spend before a drop of that honey even got on him.

She knelt between his legs, her hands push-ing back the folds of his *foustanella* until he was revealed to her, the honey dipper dripping its golden offering on the tip of his very ready phallus. She looked up at him, a veritable houri with her hair gathered over one shoulder, her eyes full of emotion. She gave him a slow smile before she bent and took him with her mouth.

Her tongue moved over his weeping tip and Brennan knew he was going to die. From pleasure. He could see his tombstone now: Brennan Alexander Carr dead at thirty from extensive pleasure. He'd been taken like this before, by women reputed to have great skill in the art of fellatio, but nothing rivalled Patra in these exquisite moments.

It occurred to him vaguely in some small, detached portion of his mind that could still process thought it was because the act *mattered* to her. She was not performing for him, not going through some technical routine that had been done perhaps countless times before. This was for him alone.

Patra's hand cupped his balls, her tongue trailing down the intimate length of him, her mouth moving around him, alternately licking at him, sucking at him, in a most decadent rhythm. His muscles clenched, tightness building on intensity. His hands anchored in the silky depths of her hair, his body gathering itself for a final, surging release. He groaned, an incoherent sound, part-warning, part-overwhelmed helplessness as the pleasure took him. Patra held him in her hand, letting him pulse and spend in the warmth of her grip.

He felt both vulnerable and powerful in the moments that followed. Physically, he lay slumped on his blanket, exposed and drained in the most satiated of ways, never mind that he couldn't have lifted a finger to defend himself if he'd had to. Maybe, he'd have been able to manage something. He'd like to think so. But mentally he was strong, empowered by the dark liquid of Patra's gaze, the reverence in her eyes when she looked up at him. There was still a journey to be faced. They would leave for England tomorrow, but he would face it with her beside him just as he would face the years of his life. He would never be alone again. He would be loved always.

Epilogue

Dover, England—one year later

Lucifer's bloody balls! They were going to be late for their own farewell breakfast. Brennan leaned out of the carriage in irritation and surveyed the scene ahead of them. A dray had overturned, blocking the road outside the Antwerp Hotel.

'I told you we should have left earlier,' Patra teased with a coy smile, poking her head out to see the wreck.

Brennan laughed and sat back in his seat. 'Told me, did you? You weren't protesting that hard. As I recall, you were the one who started it, you with your wicked hand under the blankets.' They probably shouldn't have indulged themselves one more time, but it was hard to resist when one's wife was so very *giving*.

Wife. It had been a year and he still loved the feel of that, of knowing she was his. Today, they were going home to Kardamyli, to start their life there together, one year and *two* weddings later. His grandfather the earl had insisted on doing it 'right' in an English church. All the Carrs had been married at St George's, Brennan was to be no exception. It had taken five months, most of the winter, to plan and his grandfather had spared no expense, turning the purse strings over to Brennan's mother. By English standards, the wedding had been a success; rose petals and yards of silk galore. The event had been the talk of the early 1838 Season. Patra had looked magnificent in his grandmother's wedding gown, inspiring summer brides to rummage old family trunks for heirloom gowns of their own.

Although Brennan far preferred his wedding in Kardamyli, there had been one advantage in all the planning. It had bought his friends time to make the journey. Nolan and Gianna were already in England, but Haviland

and Alyssandra had come from Paris. Archer and Elisabeta had come from Siena. They had come to see him marry Patra and they'd stayed for the first part of the Season, too. For Haviland and Archer, it was the first time they'd been back since their own marriages.

Now it was time for all of them to go home. The others were leaving today, as well. Like him, they'd stayed long enough to assure themselves home was elsewhere. For him, home was in Greece, in a little whitewashed house with blue shutters. He could hardly wait to get there, but it seemed traffic had conspired against him.

Brennan glanced over at Patra, a single thought passing between them unspoken. 'Are you thinking what I'm thinking?' Patra gave him a knowing smile. It was all the permission he needed. He grabbed her hand and flung open the carriage door. 'We're going to have to make a run for it.'

It was almost déjà vu, running through the dawn streets like this, racing the clock. He had done this before. Almost. There were some considerable improvements this time around.

There were no men chasing him with pistols for starters. Patra laughed as they ran, a clock somewhere in the city striking the hour. They were officially late. Haviland, Archer and Nolan would never let him live it down.

They were both flushed when they reached the pier where their yacht was tied, a wedding present from his grandfather. It would carry them past Spain and into the Mediterranean at record speed, courtesy of Sutton designs.

Applause broke out from the rail and Brennan sighted his friends, already on board and waiting for breakfast. 'You're late. It's nice to see some things never change,' Nolan called out, as Archer reluctantly handed over pound notes.

Brennan laughed. 'Did you lose again, Archer? As long I've known you, you have yet to win a bet with that man.'

Breakfast was laid out on the deck, making the most of the June sun and Brennan fixed himself a heaping plate. Everyone was in good spirits, talking about plans for when they got home. His friends were as eager as he was to get back to real life. Haviland and Alyssandra had plans to expand their fencing *salle* in Paris to accommodate their growing clientele. Nolan and Gianna had purchased a second home, this one in London, for wayward boys. Archer and Elisabeta had new foals to raise, and, Archer disclosed, with a wink, a baby to welcome next winter. They'd just learned of it and were now doubly eager to reach Siena.

Brennan looked at the happiness around the table. Each of them had made peace with their families and their decisions in their own ways as he had. His parents were who they were. He couldn't change them, but he could change himself. He'd learned he was responsible for his own happiness and he was embracing that responsibility wholeheartedly.

Plates emptied. Conversation dwindled. The yacht captain approached the table, reluctant to break up the party. 'We should be setting out soon, Mr Carr.'

There was a burst of renewed energy as everyone complimented the yacht, a fast new prototype out of the renowned Sutton Yacht Works, a company that had become quite the scandal in the last few weeks, especially since the new owner, Elise Sutton, had recently eloped with the Scourge of Gibraltar, Dorian Rowland, after a hair-raising sailing race against the once-unbeatable Phantasm.

'Don't you know any reputable people, Bren?' Nolan joked.

Brennan cocked his head in thought. 'I know you. Oh, wait. No, I guess not,' he joked, but the inevitable could not be put off much longer. It was time to go. As excited as he was to go home, it would be hard to leave—not England, he knew where his home was. But it would be hard to leave his friends. Archer and Haviland would set out today, too, on different boats, in different directions: Haviland and Alyssandra to Calais, Archer and Elisabeta to Ostend.

The group moved towards the gangplank and Brennan and Patra met each of them with hugs and well wishes for the wives that had made his friends so happy. Brennan embraced each of his friends, thickness in his throat. 'Haviland, thank you for always looking out for me at school even when I was an underclassman and for teaching me swords. It has, unfortunately, come in handy. I think you made me finer than I might otherwise have been.' He turned to Archer. 'Without your excellent riding instructions over the years, such as how to leap on to a running horse, I might have missed the boat two years ago in more ways than one. I would never have met the woman who showed me how to live and how to love.'

Nolan came last, unusually quiet. The two of them had become close on the tour, the only ones who had gone on to Venice together. Brennan had been the only one in Verona when Nolan had married Gianna on the run. It was a tribute to the new depth of their friendship that Nolan was rendered speechless. 'Perhaps I owe you the most, dear friend,' Brennan said loud enough for everyone to hear. 'Thank you for fighting a duel that got us kicked out of the country.' There was some general laughter and Brennan grinned, holding his friend close, letting his embrace say what words could not—that he owed Nolan far more than that. Nolan would understand.

The gangplank was lifted and the anchor

chain began to roll up. Patra looped her arms around his waist as the sleek yacht edged away from the pier, from his friends. Brennan raised an arm once in farewell. He knew they would do him the honour of standing there until he was out of sight. 'You will miss them,' she said softly.

'I don't know when I'll see them again.'

'You will,' Patra reassured him with a kiss. 'We have a fast boat and the world is changing, distances are getting smaller. Anything is possible when love is present.' She drew his hand down over her belly.

'Anything?' Brennan's breath caught at the implication.

'Anything. Even a playmate for Archer and Elisabeta's baby,' she whispered.

The captain approached discreetly with two champagne-filled glasses. Patra took them from him and gave one to Brennan. 'I thought a toast might be in order. Sometimes it makes farewells easier.'

Brennan raised his glass to the shore, to his friends, letting the sun catch the golden liquid. 'Here's to four rakes on tour, who managed to take Europe by storm and live happily ever after.'

Farewells didn't have to be goodbyes. They could be gateways to the future.

* * * * *

MILLS & BOON®

HISTORICAL

AWAKEN THE ROMANCE OF THE PAST

A sneak peek at next month's titles...

In stores from 24th March 2016:

- **The Widow and the Sheikh** – Marguerite Kaye
- **Return of the Runaway** – Sarah Mallory
- **Saved by Scandal's Heir** – Janice Preston
- **Forbidden Nights with the Viscount** – Julia Justiss
- **Bound by One Scandalous Night** – Diane Gaston
- **Western Spring Weddings** – Lynna Banning

Available at WHSmith, Tesco, Asda, Eason, Amazon and Apple

Just can't wait?
Buy our books online a month before they hit the shops!
visit www.millsandboon.co.uk

These books are also available in eBook format!

MILLS & BOON®

Helen Bianchin v Regency Collection!

0316_MB520